THESE SCANDALOUS STREETS

THESE SCANDALOUS STREETS
A Novel By Tranay Adams

THESE SCANDALOUS STREETS

These Scandalous Streets

Copyright © 2015 Tranay Adams. All rights reserved.

Warning: The unauthorized reproduction or distribution of this work is illegal. Criminal copyright infringement, including infringement without monetary gain, is investigated by FBI and is punishable by up to five (5) years in federal prison and a fine of $250,000.

All names, characters, and incidents depicted in this book are products of the author's imagination or are used fictitiously. Any resemblance to actual events, locales, organizations, or persons, living or dead, is entirely coincidental, and beyond the intent of the author and publisher.

No part of this book may be reproduced or transmitted in any form or by any means, electronic or mechanical, including photocopying, recording, or by any information storage and retrieval system, without permission in writing from the publisher.

These Scandalous Streets/ Tranay Adams-1st ed.
© 2015
Editor: Jasmine Devonish
Format: Tranay Adams
Publisher: Dope Readz Presents

THESE SCANDALOUS STREETS

THESE SCANDALOUS STREETS

ACKNOWLEDGEMENTS

I would first and foremost like to thank my supporters who are MY FAMILY. I love you all through life and past death. I cannot thank you enough for all the love that you all show the Inkpen Pimp.

Shouts out to Forever Redd for encouraging me to do my thang solo. I appreciate yo' words and friendship. Salute.

Thank you to Sunny Giovanni and Jasmine Devonish for helping me put this project together. I am especially blessed to have you both as friends of mine.

To my Queen, whomever you are, protect me from myself and I'll protect you from this world.

This my sixth joint, Let's get it.

THESE SCANDALOUS STREETS

THESE SCANDALOUS STREETS

Chapter One

"Bulletproof loveeeee…they can't break it, there's no mistaking/bulletproof loveeeee…it can't be faded, baby, we gone make it…"

Treasure Gold crooned the lyrics to one of her most memorable songs to her audience at her sold out concert in Madison Square Garden. She sung the vocals with so much passion that she had to have experienced a love that strong some time ago. She held her microphone out to the audience for them to finish the lyrics to the song, and they did. The audience was a sea of tear stained faces of women of different ages and ethnicities. They felt the words of the song; they were heartfelt, thought provoking and powerful like a sermon from a pastor.

Keith nodded his head to Treasure's infectious singing over the tantalizing track. He was a tall, caramel complexion man with hazel eyes, about fifty years old. He rocked a thin goatee and gold loop earrings. His attire was a gray suit and a black turtleneck. He was Treasure and Showtime's armed bodyguard.

"Haa! Haa!"

Showtime fogged the huge diamond of his platinum pinky ring and brushing it off on his shirt. He had a brown hue and a baldhead that shined like a polished bowling ball. His muscular toned body fitted a violet suit which he wore a black silk shirt underneath that was unbuttoned to show his chiseled chest and the platinum and diamond crucifix that rested upon it. In his suit and Italian Mauri gators he looked every bit of the C.E.O of the multimillion dollar recording label, Big Willie records, but outside of business he was what gangster rappers often claimed to be on their album.

THESE SCANDALOUS STREETS

The beat of *Bulletproof Love* was cut and all that could be heard was the beat patterned clapping of the audience as they sung Treasure's song along with her. She wailed like a young Patty Labelle. Her eyes brimmed with tears that threatened to trickle as she thought about her late boyfriend, Trip, who was murdered in a drive by a few years ago at a friend's barbeque. His death brought her both great sadness and pain.

Treasure finished her performance and a little boy sitting on his father's shoulders passed her a bouquet of red roses.

"Hear you go, Treasure." He smiled.

"Thank you, sweetheart." She kissed the seven year old boy on the cheek and he blushed.

"Dad, dad, she kissed me!" he blushed and held his cheek, not able to believe his crush had kissed him.

Treasure stood erect, cradling the bouquet of beautiful long stemmed roses. She gave her audience a breathtaking pearly white smile and bowed.

"Treasure, you're so pretty!" one woman yelled.

"I'm your biggest fan." Another one yelled.

"I have all of your albums!" a third said after that one.

"I love you, Treasure!" a fourth declared.

"I love you, too!" She kissed her palm and blew a kiss to the teenage boy out in the audience. He caught the kiss and beamed brightly. She then bowed at the waist and waved as she headed off of the stage. It was then that she let herself go a little, allowing the tears to roll down her cheeks. Coming down the small staircase that was connected to the stage, she wiped her wet face with the back of her hand.

"You okay?" Showtime frowned, seeing her damp cheeks.

"Yeah, I'm fine, just a little tired." She lied, but he wasn't going to press it.

THESE SCANDALOUS STREETS

"Well, your set is finished, we can roll out. I will have the driver pull around out back." He pulled his cell phone from within his suit.

"Alright, let me use the rest room before we leave. Hold these for me." She handed him the bouquet of roses and sauntered off with a little pep in her step as she hurried away; her black high heel Christian Louboutin's clicking on the floor loudly.

Tawk! Tawk! Tawk! Tawk!

Showtime watched the sway of his multiplatinum artist's bodacious ass as she made her way to the women's restroom. He smiled and showcased his gold capped fangs, shaking his head like it was a damn shame that a woman like her had such a nice butt.

"Umm uh, Lord have mercy." He narrowed his eyes and bit down on his bottom lip. He then turned to Keith, placing his jeweled hand on his shoulder. "Hold lil' momma down."

Keith was staring at Treasure's apple bottom, too. He crossed his heart and kissed his fingers before following her. *Oh, booty is a beautiful thing!*

Treasure bent the corner into the women's restroom with Keith right on her heels. She spun around putting her hand on his chest.

"Hold up," her brows furrowed. "Where you think you're going, negro?"

"Show told me to watch your back, and since I gotta piss anyway, I figured…" He smiled as he trailed off, looking her up and down like he was a hungry dog and she was a raw T-bone steak.

"Keith," Treasure began. "You done lost yo' damn mind if you think yo' perverted ass is walking into this restroom with me. You got me fucked up nigga, you know betta."

THESE SCANDALOUS STREETS

"But I'm in a tight," he lied, eyeing her seductively. He always cracked for the ass and she always shot him down. She wasn't fucking with him but he never seemed to get the point.

Treasure looked him up and down with an expression that read as *Do you really think I'm falling for that shit?*

"Nigga, please. I'm surprised some broad let you pump five kids in her with that tired ass game." She shook her head and twisted her lips. "I told you, Keith, you're an old man. You wouldn't know how to act if I were to let you taste this pu-nanny." She patted that slice of heaven between her legs and smiled, sliding her tongue over her top row of teeth.

He shrugged and said, "Gimmie a taste and find out."

She laughed. "Pig," she called him before shoving him aside and disappearing inside of the restroom.

He leaned up against the side of the women's restroom door, daydreaming about how sweet Treasure's pussy must taste as he stared up at the ceiling smiling.

In the restroom, Treasure laid the paper seat-protector over the toilet seat. She hurriedly pulled down her spandex leggings and sat down, relieving her bladder. "Whew." She relaxed, slumping her shoulders and lowering her eyes. She'd been in a tight since she was on stage. Treasure looked around at the stall's walls which were decorated with graffiti. She pulled out an ink pen and was about to add her own insignia. That's when she heard the door locking and saw someone walk past the opening of the stall door.

Her brows crinkled and she narrowed her eyes. "Keith, I'm not playing with you, get cho ass outta here!" She yelled. Hearing shuffling around in the neighboring stall, her head snapped to it. "Keith, on my momma, I'ma fuck you up and have Showtime fire your country ass!"

THESE SCANDALOUS STREETS

The wall of the neighboring stall rattled violently, scaring her. She hopped up, wiping herself and flushing the commode. She ran from out of the stall and a strong hand grabbed her by the arm, slinging her to the floor. Treasure hit the tiled surface and bumped the back of her skull. Grimacing, she touched the back of her head and withdrew bloody finger tips. Through her blurry vision she saw a distorted image of what she believed was a man advancing toward her. Her 20/20 came into focus and she saw him clearly. He was a stocky, dark skinned cat with a shaved head and salt & pepper chin stubble. Alongside his face was a tattoo he'd done himself while on lock in big sloppy cursive letters *Treasure*. He had toned arms, and rock hard pecks and abs. The nigga was built like The Rock. His attire was a black T-shirt with an image of *Treasure Gold* singing on stage. Over that he wore a necklace that held onto a thin, clear framed picture of him and her at an autograph signing.

"You'z a cold bitch, Treas'," he began. "A nigga just did fifteen months for a strap I was using to protect your mu'fucking ass! And you don't visit, accept my calls, write me back, or none of that shit!"

He paced the floor, smacking his forehead with his palms.

Smack! Smack! Smack!

"What?" Treasure frowned, backpedaling on her hands and the heels of her shoes. "Who the fuck are you?"

"I'm willing to work things out for lil' man's sake, but we're going to have to go to couples counseling or something." He spoke seriously, looking like every bit of the fucking nut case that he was.

"Oh, my God, this nigga is crazy." Her eyes widen with terror and her jaw dropped. "Keith! Help me!" she screamed, backpedaling faster and bumping up against the wall.

THESE SCANDALOUS STREETS

The restroom door rattled violently from powerful kicks as Keith attempted to get in.

"Fuck is going on in there?" She heard Keith's voice boom from the opposite side of the door.

"What's going on?" Showtime asked.

"Treasure's in trouble, man," Keith told him. "Someone's in there with her."

"Shit." The door rattled some more, but the combined efforts of Keith and Showtime just wasn't enough to get the goddamn thing open.

"We need more man power! Y'all niggaz come on!" Showtime told the rest of his entourage.

"Oh, so it's like that?" the stalker asked Treasure, disappointedly. In his mind his crazy ass thought they were really in a relationship. "You gon' act like you don't even know a brotha now, huh? That's fucked up." He pulled her to her feet by her arm, with an iron grip. "I know what it is! You've been fucking somebody else since I've been gone, haven't chu? Keep that shit a hunnit. You been giving up my pussy?" he screamed on her with madness in his eyes, breath smelling like cigarettes and something with onions. This nigga had Treasure shook to the core. She was damn near trembling. "It may be on you but this is mine!" he smacked his calloused hand against her twat and squeezed.

"Get the fuck off of me!" she yelled and punched him in the eye, causing him to stagger back and clutch his shit. His head slowly rose and he laughed hard and manically.

"Hahahahahaha!"

This caused Treasure to quiver with fear; she was literally trembling all over.

Her stalker looked into terrified eyes and said, "Uhh huh, that's what I'm tom 'bout, that's that thug passion right there!" his hand slid down his chiseled six pack and slipped

THESE SCANDALOUS STREETS

into his jeans. He stroked his meat to hardness as he licked his lips, approaching her. "You always were a sucker for rough sex."

Crack!

Treasure spun around in a 180 degree turn and hit the floor, landing on her knees and hands. She blinked her eyes as if she didn't know where she was. She was dizzy and her nose and mouth were trickling blood, making a small puddle below her chin.

"Aaaahh." She moaned. She tried to get up but kept on falling back down before she could plant her heel firmly on the linoleum.

"This is gon' be good." The whack job unbuckled his belt. "A nigga just came home and I need some pussy to get my mind right." His jeans dropped to the floor and he pulled down his briefs, exposing his long, thick donkey like dick.

Treasure looked over her shoulder at him, seeing that he was now nude, she screamed, "Help! Helppp! Somebody help me, pleeeease!"

The crazy nigga straddled her and as he held down both her wrists, he began to place hickeys on her neck. "Mmmm."

Sloshing and sucking filled her ears as he sucked on her neck like a wet leech, nibbling on her flesh. His body odor was a combination of must and cheap cologne that assaulted her nasal passages and made her gag. Her eyebrows arched and her nose scrunched up.

"Ahhhh!" she screamed at the top of her lungs with her head pressed back against the floor, with him still feasting on her neck. She whipped her head from left to right and thrashed her legs, the heels of her shoes leaving several black streaks on the floor. Desperately, she tried to shake off his advances, but her efforts were futile.

THESE SCANDALOUS STREETS

"'Nough of this foreplay shit, a nigga want some ass!" With a grunt, he ripped open her blouse, sending buttons flying everywhere and exposing her melon like breasts. *Schhhrippp!* He stripped the Victoria Secret bra from her with a strong yank, tossing it aside. Treasure scratched and clawed at his eyes, leaving crimson streaks over his face.

Bwap!

A right to the jaw left her groaning and barely conscious.

"Aaaaa." She groaned, her head bobbling about loosely.

"Mmmmm." The man sucked on her breasts like a starving baby. He pulled down her spandex leggings and panties. He spat in his palm and used the saliva to lubricate his manhood, gliding his hand up and down his member.

"This shit isn't working," Showtime said from behind the restroom door. "You gon' have to blast it open."

"Alright, step aside." Keith ordered.

Choot! Choot! Choot! Choot! Choot!

A ring of bullet holes spat out the wood surrounding the door handle of the restroom door. The chunk of wood dropped to the floor. *Boom!* Keith kicked that bitch wide open, his hand gripping a smoking, silenced .45. He and the rest of the entourage poured inside over the threshold.

"Get offa her, get cho ass up!" One of them shouted, as they snatched the stalker up from Treasure just as he was about to penetrate her. They drug him to the corner where they proceeded to stomp and kick him.

Whack! Crack! Wop! Boop!

Treasure ran into Showtime's arms, sobbing into the breast of his suit. He rubbed her back soothingly, consoling her.

"Shhh, it's gonna be all right, we're here now."

Over her shoulder he watched as his crew administered a brutal beating that left smears of blood on the floor. He

THESE SCANDALOUS STREETS

didn't even cringe seeing his crew give Treasure's stalker that act right.

"Hoe ass nigga!" one of the entourage member's stomped Treasure's stalker on the temple.

"Y'all niggaz get the fuck outta the way!" Keith ordered the crew with a sway of his gun. He was heated and ready to introduce dude to the afterlife.

The men gave him a wide berth, leaving the deranged stalker bloody faced and lumped up like The Elephant Man. He had what was called a pumpkin head when your dome had swollen after a severe beat down. Both that nigga'z eyes were swollen shut and his left cheek was swelling. He was fucked up. Showtime's people really gave homie that work. His own mother wouldn't recognize him.

"I—I—I love her," he croaked, reaching out. "We're married."

Keith stuck his silenced .45 into the stalker's mouth causing him to gag. "Gahhh!"

"Til' death do you part," his eyebrows lowered and his eyes darkened. He squared his jaws and they throbbed, before pulling the trigger.

Choot!

The gun jumped in his hand as it fired, smoke billowed out of the crazy man's grill. His head jerked violently as blood, brain fragments, and pieces of skull splattered over the walls, floor, and the leg of the killer's pants.

Keith rose to his feet, straightening his suit and admiring his handiwork.

"Damn, Keith, I wish you wouldn't have done the nigga in here." Showtime stepped forth, looking over the fresh cadaver who had a large hole at the back of his noodle. "We're in Madison Square Garden; there's security and surveillance cameras everywhere, baby."

THESE SCANDALOUS STREETS

The killer shrugged and holstered his head bussa. "Well, fix this how you fix everything else, nigga."

Showtime shot Keith a dirty look. He mumbled something under his breath as he pulled out his cell phone and punched in a number. The device rang twice before someone answered.

"Hey, what's up, fam? This Show." He spoke into his cellular. "I gotta lil' mess I need cleaned up. Yeah, I know y'all quote, nigga. How long we been doing business? I'm at Madison Square Garden. Mannnn, y'all just get your asses over here. One hundred." He disconnected the call and deposited it inside of his suit. He pulled out a bankroll and turned to the refrigerator size man in his entourage.

"Jumbo, I want you to find out who's watching the monitors for the security cameras. Lay this paper on them and get that surveillance tape. Without it, Keith is looking at a murder rap and we'll be going down as accessories." He tossed the man the bankroll of dead presidents. "The rest of y'all watch the door and make sure no one comes in here. I'm gonna put Treasure in the car and send her to the house. Scrub and Bubbles should be here in a sec to dispose of our friend there." He threw his head toward the dead ass nigga sprawled on the linoleum. He then turned to Keith, holding out his hand. "Gimmie yo' strap."

"For what?" Keith frowned and coiled his neck.

"Do you really wanna be caught out here with the murder weapon if Jake gets here before Scrub and his brother do?" He looked at him with a raised eyebrow.

"Shit, man, this is my favorite gun," Keith complained, stomping his Fennix leather shoe. He pulled his burner from its holster and handed it to Showtime who tucked it into the small of his back.

THESE SCANDALOUS STREETS

"Come on, Treasure," Showtime took her under his arm and headed out of the restroom.

***

Showtime opened the backdoor of the stretched Mercedes Benz and deposited Treasure into the backseat. Removing his handkerchief, he wiped the head bussa clean of finger prints and stashed it into a secret compartment.

"You okay, kid?" he asked Treasure, who was now behind big Chanel shades that covered most of her face. She nodded yes. "Alright, I'm gon'call this doctor friend of mine and have 'em come to the house to check you out."

"Nah, I'm good. No doctors." She told him, pouring up a drink.

"You sure, didn't he?"

Her head snapped in his direction, with attitude. Her forehead wrinkled. "No!"

"Alright, then," He slammed the door shut and went about his business. The limousine resurrected and pulled away with the songstress drinking like a fish. This had been one of the scariest nights of her life and she wanted to become numb to it.

***

Back at Showtime's mansion, inside Treasure's bathroom, hot water sprayed from the shower nozzle creating steam that fogged the bathroom mirror. She wiped the mirror with her hand, revealing her reflection in it. She gave herself the once over, seeing her eye had blackened and swelled. She poked at it and winced.

THESE SCANDALOUS STREETS

"Ouch." Staring at her reflection, her eyes pooled with tears and cascaded down her face. She lay in a fetal position on the floor, cradling her naked body and sobbing. Finally alone, she was free to breakdown.

"Haa! Haa! Haa!" her body shuddered as she hugged her knees to her chest, making an ugly face, head bobbing. "Ah, haa, haa, haa!"

Chapter Two

Tyson lay on the bottom bunk inside of his cell staring at the bars. His torso was wrapped in two inches of news paper and two prison made knives known as Bone Crushers were concealed inside the sleeves of his shirt. His eyelids were heavy, but he didn't dare to blink them; some of Grief's goons could rush into his house at any time and give both him and his cousin a stabbing as brutal as the one Montoya Santana got in *American Me*. He couldn't have that so he knew he had to stay on point in that bitch.

"Ty?" Cody called from the top bunk where he was wiping his dripping nose with the back of his hand, having just snorted the last of his secret stash of heroin. The way he blinked his moist eyes and coughed it seemed like he was coming down with the flu but that wasn't further from the truth. He was supposed to have been sleep while Tyson took first watch, but he'd spent most of the night getting high and trying to forget about the seriousness of his situation. Boy, was he up Shit's Creek without a paddle.

"What?"

He turned over on his side. "You sleep?"

"Nigga, if I were sleep we'd both be dead right now."

Cody blew hard, "I really fucked up this time, huh?"

"Royally." Tyson answered.

About two years ago Cody had gotten busted for sticking up a liquor store. Being that it was his first offense he was offered three years which he took and was sent straight to the big house. While on lock he'd gotten hooked on heroin, using the drug to escape his harsh reality. At first he supplied his habit by robbing and extorting inmates weaker than him, but then that well ran dry and he made the mistake of copping some heroin from Grief, the shot-caller of the Bay

THESE SCANDALOUS STREETS

area niggaz in the pen, on consignment knowing well he hadn't had any gwap to pay for it. Once the shot caller came to the realization that he had copped his dope on ass, he didn't waste any time putting a hit out on him and anybody willing to stand next to him. Outnumbered, Cody's crew abandoned him, leaving his relative to hold him down.

"My bad, Blood," Cody sat up in bed and brought his hands down his face, exhaling. "Look, I'ma tell this nigga Grief this shit ain't got nothing to do with you. If I get handled then I get handle. I'm sorry for bringing you into my bullshit, man." He jumped down from the top bunk and carried his 6 foot frame over to the sink. After giving himself the once over in the mirror he cupped his hands under the running faucet and splashed water on his face. He stared at his reflection as the water rolled and dripped from his bronze self. He was only twenty four, but his rock star lifestyle and drugs made him damn near twice his age.

Tyson looked to the wall beside his bunk and saw a cockroach making its way toward the floor. He placed his hand on the wall and the brown insect crawled up his fingers. He rotated his hand as the roach traveled around his chocolate mitt, desperately trying to find some place to go. Amused, the thug brought his left-hand beside his right and the bug transferred over to it.

As he watched the roach make its journey over his hands, he thought long and hard about Cody's situation. His younger kin was a world-class fuck up. A knucklehead that lived to do mischief; his middle name was *Trouble*. But for as much as a screw up as he was, his narrow ass was still family. He was his first cousin and his mother's younger sister's only son. Cody, Tyson and his older brother Moon all grew up together, so their union was more like brothers, than cousins.

THESE SCANDALOUS STREETS

"Shut that shit up, Cody, we family. We protect our own. True, you're the one that fucked up, but we gon' face this shit together."

"I feel you, but chu getting outta here in the next couple of days. And if something were to happen to you, I just don't want that shit on my conscience, Blood. What the fuck would I tell Uncle Henry, huh?" he asked as he took off his shirt revealing a collage of body art. Most noticeably the naked woman on his chest with a red bandana over the lower half of her face holding two smoking revolvers; *RTBG* was on her right-breast.

"Guess you should have thought about that before you ran off with that Bay nigga'z dope," Tyson scolded, making Cody feel even worse about his situation. He shook his head as he passed the cockroach from one hand to the other. He could have beat his relative's ass for the situation that he'd put him in two days before he was released from that shithole.

Two days, just two days before I walk and here he comes with this shit, he sighed and shook his head, looking at his cousin. *Goddamn you, Cody.*

Cody took the red band from around his thick dreadlocks and shook them loose. They went flying every which way before eventually hanging over his shoulders. He then pulled them back up, wrapping them up with the band. "I'ma dead man walking, either way you look at it, my nigga," he said as he did pushups on the floor. "Once you walk from behind these walls…it's buzzards for me, dawg. Ain't gon' be nobody here to watch a young nigga'z back. That old head gon' send half the prison in here for my skinny black ass; they might get me but before I go I'ma give a few of them mothafuckaz something to remember me by. They may kill me but they gon' feel me when I'm gone, ya dig?"

THESE SCANDALOUS STREETS

"Don't trip, you let me worry about that," Tyson told him as he placed his hand on the wall and let the cockroach crawl from his hand into a crack in the wall. "It's your shift," he placed his hands on his stomach and closed his eyes. Cody pulled his Bone Crusher from underneath his pillow and stood guard at the bars.

"Yo, Cody?"

"What up, Ty?" he replied, focusing through the bars.

"If I wake up dead tomorrow, remind me to kill you."

Cody smirked, "Alright."

"I love you, dumbass." He shut his eyes and grinned.

"I love you, too."

***

The next morning Cody and Tyson ate breakfast and headed out onto the yard. They could feel the stares of the other convicts as they treaded across the ground watching, waiting. Their eyes never seemed to stay still as they were on the move, keeping their hands near the Bone Crushers stashed on their waists.

"Keep close," Tyson said to his cousin in a hush tone, watching the yard and flipping a razor blade over in his mouth, it appeared as if he was sucking on a piece of candy. "If it pops off then we go down swinging, you hear me?" he told Cody. He nodded as he walked beside his relative, surveying his surroundings.

The cousins were en route to the area of the yard that Grief and the rest of the Bay area cats populated. They spotted the OG playing handball with one of his minions, he was oblivious to the presence of his adversaries but he didn't have to be. He had eyes and ears everywhere, before the

THESE SCANDALOUS STREETS

cousins got within ten feet of the shot-caller they were swarmed from all sides by his minions.

No retreat, no surrender, Tyson thought, his eyes shifting around to all of the hard faces of the larcenous men surrounding them. He and Cody stood back to back, hearts racing, adrenaline pumping madly. Here was the time, here was the place. The shit was about to go down.

Snikt! Snikt! Tyson drew seven inches of Death from his waist. His relative was right behind him, drawing steel of his own. They frowned and tightened their jaws, flexing the muscles in their faces. The ring of bodies slowly began closing around them, making them feel claustrophobic, sucking in all of the air from around them. They took in the murderous glares of the impending threats; some of them were the more reputable killers that the facility had to offer. So they knew any sudden movement could end with blood spilling onto the dirt patched lawn.

Here we go, Tyson's head snapped from left to right, veins forming on the top of his hand as he clutched his weapon tighter, gritting his teeth. Cody matched his cousin's intensity. *Hoe ass nigga* was a small town up the road and he didn't plan on visiting any time soon.

Thump-Thump! Thump-Thump! Thump-Thump!

Their heart rates amped and perspiration brought forth the sweat on their faces.

"Remember what I said, Cody, *if we go down then we'll go down swinging*," Tyson reminded his kin as they stared down their combatants, who were moving to draw their bangers as well.

"I gotchu," Cody replied, staring down the men also. He was ready and waiting. If he went down then he was going to take a couple of them bitch ass niggaz with him.

THESE SCANDALOUS STREETS

"I'll tell ya, mane, you and your cousin have got to be two of the dumbest mu'fuckaz I've ever laid eyes on; what kinda niggaz waltz right up to the lion and sticks their heads in its mouth?" Whispers smiled wickedly, showcasing his coffee stained teeth. He spoke with a soft, raspy voice that wasn't any more than a whisper due to the damage to his vocal cords. He shook his head shamefully and took a sip of his steaming cup of coffee. The six foot two, lanky man wore a blue beanie over his brows and his jean jacket buttoned to the top. All of Grief's minions possessed weapons of their own except for him. He was their second in command and he didn't get his hands dirty nearly as much as he used to. Nah, he'd proven his worth plenty of times. Now he got to kick up his feet and watch the rest of the wolves put in work which was something he thoroughly enjoyed.

"We didn't come here looking for trouble. We just wanna talk to old head. I've gotta business proposition for 'em." Tyson told him.

Whispers laughed and shook his head, "Homie, the time for talking has passed. Grief wants that paypa, and since your people doesn't have it. We gon' take it out his ass!" he sneered with his forehead creased and jaws rigid.

When Grief's goons moved to butcher Tyson and Cody, he made his move with blinding speed. He smacked the cup of coffee out of Whispers' hand, the hot liquid splashed into his face, sizzling his skin.

Sssssssssss!

"Arghhhhhhhh!" He made a blood curdling scream and grabbed for his stinging face. "Ooof!" Tyson kicked him in his balls and he doubled over clutching his precious jewels.

"Huuuu!" the minion's eyes bugged and his mouth shot open when the thug karate chopped him in his throat causing him to drop his shank to the ground. His face registered the devastation of the assault. He went to reach for his paining neck. *Bwap!* He was kicked so hard in the chest that the impact sent him flying backwards with his legs up in the air and he came crashing down along with his flailing arms. Seeing the shadow of someone sneaking up behind him with something sharp held above his head on the ground, Tyson whipped around just as the minion was bringing the long, jagged shank down. He caught the man's wrist and twisted it upward. *Snap!* He broke his wrist and caused him to howl like a wounded dog while dropping his weapon. Still holding his wrist, he swung around leaving his back to him and brought his locked arm down over his shoulder with a grunt. *Poppp!* The bone snapped up, breaking through the flesh of the skin.

"Arghhhh!" his eyes flashed pain and his mouth stretched wide open, showcasing his missing teeth. He released the man and he hunched over, only to receive a round house kick to the face. *Woowap!* The blow flipped him over, landing him on his stomach. The thug landed on his feet with his legs apart, still gripping his Bone Crusher. When he heard someone running up behind him yelling, he swung around and found Whispers charging him with the biggest, longest piece of steel he'd ever seen in all of his years in prison. He flipped his weapon over in his palm, and took a stance, narrowing his eyes at the raging brute. Suddenly, he threw the shank as hard as he could; it spun rapidly in circles becoming a blur while en route.

Thock!

"Gahhh!" Whispers' head snapped back as he screamed at the top of his lungs, veins bulging up his neck and forehead. He grabbed the handle of the weapon as he dropped to the ground; he looked down at it frighteningly with quivering lips.

THESE SCANDALOUS STREETS

Tyson looked up and saw his cousin tussling over a shank with one of the goons, while another one was sneakily approaching him from behind, long sharp metal in his grip ready to pierce a major artery. He hurriedly stalked forth, chopping Whispers in the back of neck, knocking him out cold before the side of his face met the dirt. Tyson's stalking turned into a full blown sprint, leaping into the air like he was attempting to fly out of a window; he tackled the man sneaking up behind Cody. They collided with the surface and he dropped his blade. The man lay in a daze beneath him, eyes rolling up in the back of his head. Staring down at his foe angrily, he spit the razor blade out of his mouth and into his palm. He maneuvered the razor over his fingers until it was pinched between his pointer finger and thumb, shiny with his saliva. When he turned the man's neck to the side and saw his Adam's apple, he threw his hand back and squared his jaws. He was about to cut his throat when he heard the guard shout from the tower.

"Get down! Everybody get down! Get down now!" All of the convicts hit the dirt, leaving the thug sticking out like a sore thumb.

"Rock a bye ba—Uhhhh!"

Pat!

The guard in the tower coiled as he fired the shot but Tyson was tackled to the ground by what looked like a blur. The bullet bit into the ground, kicking up dust. He looked to his right and found Malakai lying beside him, breathing heavily.

"You good, homie?" he asked.

The day Tyson walked through the gates of The Belly of the Beast he was assigned to the muscle bound man who showed him the ropes. The two of them shared the same house and had developed a bond. Just when they'd become accustomed to one another, he was moved out and transferred to Cody's cell. Although he wasn't sure, he had the feeling that his cell mate had arranged for him to share the same house as his relative. Ever since then the two would see one another in passing but they didn't exchange anything more than the occasional nod of acknowledgment.

Tyson nodded his head, "Yeah, I'm straight. You all right?"

Malakai nodded.

"Why'd you do that?"

"What chu mean, my nigga? I've been watching yo' back since you were a new fish."

"Thanks, man."

"No problem."

Tyson looked over his shoulder and saw a mob of COs headed their way. He then looked to his cousin. "Cody, are you, all right?" he called out to him.

"Yeah, I'm good!" Cody yelled back, wincing, looking to the blood on the tips of his fingers. He was stabbed twice, but he'd live. He looked beyond his feet and saw the man he was tussling with. His face held a mask of pain as he held his oozing neck.

The inmates that were injured during the fight were sent straight to the infirmary, while Tyson and Malakai were escorted to their cells. Tyson thought for sure that they'd be housed in segregation, but the CO escorting him to his cell told him that Grief had pulled some strings. Although the OG was incarcerated like the rest of them his name held some weight. He was in a position of power and could make things happen; being behind the barbwire walls didn't deter that. Prison may have held him but it did nothing to his influence.

THESE SCANDALOUS STREETS

It was one o'clock in the morning when Tyson was stirred awake from his sleep from the sound of metal clinking as his barred cell was being opened by a correctional officer. He wiped the sleep from his eyes with the back of his hand, and sat up in bed.

"What's up, man?" he asked groggily.

"Grief wants to see you," was all the officer said, leading him out onto the tier and down into the mess-hall. When he crossed the threshold onto the waxed, shiny floor of the cafeteria, it was practically empty. Grief was sitting at one of the center tables and there were COs at three of the four corners of the room. After leaving Tyson with the old con, the officer who'd ushered him in took post at the empty corner of the room.

"I understand you have some business you'd like to discuss with me," the OG began, staring down at the orange as he peeled it. "Well, I'm all ears."

Tyson gave the old school gangster the once over before presenting him with a proposition. Grief was a man of onyx hue. He stood five foot seven and had a crown of snow white hair that he wore in a short tamed afro and a thick comb mustache. He sat back eating his orange as he listened to Tyson's business proposal. He'd offered to give him four cups of noodles, three Snicker bars, two cookies and half a book of stamps to settle his cousin's debt. The items went a long way in prison. Tyson felt that the deal was one too sweet to pass up. He'd thrown out the bait and he just knew the shot-caller was going to bite.

Grief cleared his throat as he wiped his mouth with a handkerchief. "That's a sweet deal, a real sweet deal." He said, bringing a smile to the young man's face. "But the time for your cousin to pay his debt through that method has passed." The smile on his face vanished. "You could offer

THESE SCANDALOUS STREETS

me a million dollars and I wouldn't take it, 'cause now it's the principal. I'm expected to make an example outta Cody, you know that. The problem is I'm making good money right now in here, and to settle another beef would mean another lockdown, something I don't need. My soldiers need to move around if they gon' make they scratch."

"Look, just tell me what I gotta do to make this right between you and my people, and I'll do it."

Tyson sat up and folded his hands on the table.

Grief massaged his chin as he thought about how the young man could rectify his cousin's situation. He leaned forward over the table and motioned for him to come closer. Hesitantly, he obliged him.

"Alright, have you heard of the R&B singer Treasure Gold?" he asked.

"You mean old girl that sings Bulletproof Love and Hold him down?" Tyson asked.

He wondered what the hell the old man knew about Treasure Gold, all he'd ever heard him rap about was Fats Domino, Billy Holiday, Sam Cook, Nat King Cole and the rest of the singers from back in the day. He used to always talk about how today's music didn't compare to the music of his generation.

"Yeah, that's her," he confirmed. "That's my baby girl, man. Anyway, she was involved in an incident up there in New York. The brotha she had working security wasn't worth a goddamn. My baby was almost violated, and Lord knows if that were to have happened..." He trailed off, balling his hands into fists and clenching his jaws. His eyes turned glassy and flashed murder. He wished that cock sucker that harmed his baby girl was locked up with him. The things he would do to him would put the killer in The Silence of The Lambs movie to shame. There weren't any doubts in Tyson's mind that the shot-caller would issue an extreme and unusual punishment to his daughter's attacker. Hell, he was in prison for the long walk for murdering the four men that had raped his wife and slit her throat.

Grief pulled himself together and continued, clearing his throat. "Pardon me; my daughter needs someone with her twenty-four hours a day, seven days a week. I don't want her to ever be alone."

"I feel you, fam. You know you can hire some off duty cops, or…"

"Nah, fuck five owe! I want chu to handle it," he commanded, pointing his finger.

"Me?" Tyson asked with a thumb to his chest.

"Yeah, you, I saw how you handled yourself out there with my boys. That was some Steven Segal type of shit. Your hands were like blurs." he mimicked his moves from earlier yesterday, looking like a kid faking martial arts moves. "I wouldn't feel comfortable with my baby being out there unless I knew she'd be with you. Now I've already got in touch with the CEO of the label, he's going to put chu on the payroll and…"

"Grief, man, I'm not a bodyguard. That's not my thing." Tyson explained.

"Oh, it will be your *thing* if you wanna keep that lil' dumbass cousin of yours outta harm's way. This is the deal, take it or leave it." Grief said seriously, with a pair of vindictive eyes.

Tyson sat back shaking his head, he blew hard. He then waved his hand and said, "Go ahead, man."

"Like I said, I've already discussed everything with Showtime, and he's gonna put chu down under his company: Big Willie Records. Since you're a felon your job title will be unarmed security guard, but never mind that. If you're going to be watching over my baby girl I want chu packing at all times."

"How long do I have to do this?" Tyson inquired.

"How long is Cody down for?" Grief asked, referring to Cody's jail time.

"He gotta pull one more bullet." *That was one year.*

"Alright, then you'll stay with Treasure until then." Tyson shook his head and massaged the bridge of his nose. He couldn't believe the shit Cody had gotten him into. "Everything should work out fine. You'll be getting paid under a legitimate business and your cousin will be okay in here. No worries. Everything will be beautiful, alright?" Tyson nodded his head. Grief pulled an envelope from out of jean jacket and handed it over to him. "That's the address and the number to Big Willie records, as well as a lil' cash."

Tyson stuffed the envelope into the pocket inside of his jacket, "Is that it?" he asked, standing to his feet. The OG's response was snapping his fingers and motioning for the CO that brought his guest in to come over. He then rose to his feet to meet the young man and extended his hand. He looked to Grief's hand and then up at him before shaking it.

"Throw in those cups of noodles and cookies and shit for the fellas. You know you and that cousin of yours did quite a number on Whispers and the gang." Grief grinned.

"Will do," Tyson smirked.

The CO lead the thug toward the exit, he had almost crossed the threshold when the OG called for his attention. "New school," Tyson turned around with a raised eyebrow like *What's up?* "If I were you I'd take good care of my baby girl, 'cause whatever fate that may befall her, your cousin will visit."

THESE SCANDALOUS STREETS

Tyson nodded his head, acknowledging the threat, and continued on out of the mess-hall with the correctional officer bringing up the rear.

THESE SCANDALOUS STREETS
Chapter Three

Bare chest, he stared up at the bars of his cell, his thick nappy beard, which made him look like he was wearing an afro on the lower half of his face, coming up and down on the floor as he did pushups. "Haa! Haa! Haa! Haa!" His hot, husky breath blew the debris masking the surface each time he came into contact with it. The muscles in his forearms, shoulders, and back flexed during the intense exercise. Malakai Williams was ripped the fuck up; his body resembled a young Arnold Schwarzenegger in his role as The Terminator. On his back was a tattoo of his late older brother, the superstar rapper, Blessyn. *Thug* Angel was tattooed across his broad shoulders while the image of his sibling was beneath it. He was bare chest and wearing heavy jewels while holding a microphone to his lips. Wings were stretched long and wide from his back. A halo was above his head. The piece was beautiful. It looked lifelike. Below it was the lyricist's date of birth and death, June 7th 1983- September 13th 2010. There wasn't a part of Malakai that wasn't covered in veins and muscles. He'd entered the prison a measly one hundred and sixty pounds. Now he was two hundred and twenty pounds of chiseled, rock solid muscle. This mothafucka was built like a tank and as sturdy as a building.

"Haa! Haa! Haa!" hot beads of sweat covered every inch of Malakai's dark chocolate form, sweat rolling down his forehead and dripping off of his brows. The droplets trickled and made small splashes on the floor, staining it wet. As soon as he finished his last set, he heard the booted feet of several correctional officers approaching and jumped to his feet in a hurry. After drying off with his undershirt, he tied it around his head to protect his skull from the beating he

THESE SCANDALOUS STREETS

believed he was in for. He then wrapped his fists up in torn bed sheets making them look like he was wearing boxing gloves with finger openings. Seeing shadows move at the corner of his eye and hearing the jingling of keys, he whipped around to the bars of his cell.

"Come on, come on, mothafucka!"

He bent his neck from left to right and then pounced from one foot to the other. The hulk of a man slammed his fist into each of his palms and flexed his fingers within the homemade boxing gloves. He knew that they may take him out but he was gone put a few of their asses on their backs. "Y'all may walk up in here but they gon' be carrying ya asses out in body bags, ya hear me? Ya hear me? You got the right mothafucka today! Come on, come on up in here!" He smacked his hand up against his chest hard which drove his voice up a few octaves. "I'ma make you my bitches, niggaz! My bitches!" Malakai began shadowboxing as the lock of his cell's door clicked open. He slipped a homemade mouth guard into his mouth and squared up for the confrontation, pouncing from one foot to other again.

He didn't know what was up but he was sure as hell going to be ready for whatever that came down on him for saving Tyson's ass. See, he knew that he should have been put in The Hole for getting himself involved in the fight that went down on the yard. But for whatever reason he was escorted back to his cell. He found this odd being that he had broken the prison's law. The first thing he thought was that Grief had handed down his death sentence for helping his enemy. Being aware of the OG's influence he knew that he had power and could send a nigga to meet his maker inside or outside of prison. Although he was well aware of the consequences for assisting Tyson and his cousin he still lent them a hand. He had convinced himself that whatever

THESE SCANDALOUS STREETS

troubles that the young convict had weren't those of his own, but seeing how close he was to being greeted by The Angel of Death he quickly erased those thoughts. See, he and Tyson had somewhat of a friendship. He was an alright dude as far as he was concerned. The brother was down to earth, smart, intelligent, funny and had a gangsta that he respected. Bottom line, he was one of those cats that you couldn't see anyone not liking. He had that personality that drew people in and made them want to be around him. And these were the reasons why Malakai had thrown himself into his mix. This wasn't the first time he'd gotten himself involved in business that wasn't his own though.

A little over eight years ago, an All Star high school basketball player by the name of Mike was gunned down and robbed for his Air Jordan's. The entire community was in an uproar and mourning due to the devastating blow his murder brought. Malakai was one of the ones that took it the hardest being that he'd bought the youngster the expensive sneakers as a gift. He couldn't get it out of his head that it was his fault that he was dead because if he wouldn't have copped them the shoes then he'd still be alive. Malakai paid for the funeral and gave the kid's mother some money to help with her bills. The night of the funeral he ordered Bizeal and Crazy, his goons, to find the cat that had laid young Mike to rest. About three hours later they were calling him with the address where they were holding him hostage. Twenty minutes later he found himself down in the basement of some abandoned building playing judge, jury, and executioner. They strapped Spud down to a table and forced a 2 x 4 between his ankles. Malakai had saw this punishment handed down in the movie Misery and he always wanted to do some fucked up shit like that to a nigga that had done some foul ass shit.

THESE SCANDALOUS STREETS

"Wait a minute, man, hold up!" Spud pleaded with glassy, terrified eyes. His head moved about, watching Malakai searching for something that would assist him in getting the job done.

"I ain't tryna hear that shit!" he hastily scanned the basement for a blunt object. A wicked smile stretched across his lips when he spotted a long rusted pipe that curled at its end. He scooped it up and turned around to his intended victim, smacking it into his palm repeatedly as he stalked in his direction. Pat! Pat! Pat! Pat! The hard metal made its noise striking his dry, palm. He lowered his head and eyebrows, staring him down menacingly, looking like the devil himself. With attentive eyes he watched him struggle against his restraints uselessly, trying desperately to escape the debt for the wrong he'd caused.

"Please, man, pleeeassse!" Spud's hoe ass screamed as loud as he could, tears jetted from the corners of his eyes along down the sides of his face.

"Nah, fuck that, you wanted the new J's, right? Well, now you've gotta pay for 'em, ain't shit free here, homeboy! That's a hunnit dollas a sneaker and that ass 'bout to pay up." Malakai had a pair of vengeful eyes as he stepped to his business, gripping the lengthy pipe like a golf club. He took the stance of a professional golfer about to swing his iron, cocking the metal around and above his head.

"Mommaaaaa!" Spud's eyelids snapped open and he bellowed loud enough to startle the deaf.

"Fourrrrrrr!" Malakai called out and swung the pipe with all of his might. It whistled through the air. Swoooof! Crrrackkk! The bitch ass nigga'z right ankle twisted all of the way around, pointing to the ground. It swelled instantly and bone shards poked up from the skin, resembling bloody spikes.

THESE SCANDALOUS STREETS

Spud looked down at his mutilated ankle and was horrified at what he witnessed with his bulging eyes, screaming like a white bitch in a scary movie. "Ahhh! Ahhhh! Ahhhhh! Ahhhhh!" his chest swelled higher and higher the louder he shrilled.

"Shut him the fuck up!" Malakai ordered, nostrils flaring, eyes darkened by hate. Bizeal snatched the beanie from off of his head and crammed it inside of his mouth, muffling his cries. "Yeahhh, oh, yeah," he licked his lips as he feasted his eyes on the last ankle. He couldn't wait to break that mothafucka. He looked up at the ceiling and spoke to the poor soul he was avenging. "This one is for you, baby boy." Malakai turned his attention back to the last ankle, moving his fingers animatedly around the pipe, grasping it. He curled the metal around and above his head, swinging it back around. Swoooof! Crrrackkk! The ankle snapped all of the way around, leaving the foot pointing to ground and trickling blood. Spud's eyes rolled to their whites and he passed out. Breathing heavily, Malakai tossed the pipe aside and it clinked on the floor.

"You want me to finish this fool?" Crazy withdrew his head bussa from off of his waist and held it near Spud's head. He looked from him to his boss, dancing a little because he was excited about ending his life on his orders.

"Nah." Malakai shook his head no. "Drop his punk ass off in the middle of his hood; let the streets know that justice has been served."

With that said, he trekked back to his Benz, climbed in and pulled off. After depositing Spud in the trunk of their ride, Crazy and Bizeal drove away to do what they were ordered. Malakai would grow to hate himself for not doing away with Spud when he had the chance. The kid pointed him out in a line up and testified in court that he was the one

THESE SCANDALOUS STREETS

that left him crippled for the rest of his life. The judge gave the hustler eight years for aggravated assault and his niggaz gave Spud eight slugs to the face. Although, he'd done hard time for dishing out his brand of justice, he'd gladly do it all over again if it meant he'd get to see homeboy suffering all over again like he did that night. He found satisfaction in believing that young Michael Tyler was resting in peace now.

The convicts in the neighboring cells stuck their small mirrors out between the bars of their cells to see the drama that was about to pop off. When they saw the guards and heard Malakai talking that shit it riled all of them up.

"Fuck them mothafuckaz up, Malakai!" one of them shouted.

"Whoop they mothafuckin' ass, homie!" another one yelled out.

"Show 'em how real gangstas are built!" a third sounded off.

A mesh of voices resonated throughout the cell block. The convicts continued to shout shit and hurl insults at the correctional officers. All this did was gas Malakai up. He was good to go now, fired up, and anxiously awaiting to get it in with them fuck-niggaz.

"Ah! Ahh! Ahhh! Ahhhhhhhh!" Malakai's eyes exploded with rage as he screamed, head vibrating with his shrilling. Saliva webbed the inside of his mouth and veins bulged at his temples and neck. He beat and pounded on his chest like a goddamn gorilla ready to set it the fuck off up in there.

The leading correctional officer pulled the cell's door open. He entered while the others stood outside of the confinement. He wore a dead serious expression, like he wasn't up for any bullshit.

"Pack your shit, you're goin' home!"

THESE SCANDALOUS STREETS

"I'm not stupid, pig! You ain't 'bout to set me up, fuck outta here!" he threw phantom punches and made noises with his mouth like a boxer would.

"I'm not for any shit! Gather your things and move it out!"

"Fuck you!"

"Alright, stay your black ass in here then." He made to walk away.

"Wait."

The guard turned around with a deep crease on his forehead, folding his arms across his chest.

"You not bullshitting me? I can go home?"

The officer nodded. Malakai relaxed, feeling the weight of his circumstances lifting from off his shoulders. He pulled the undershirt from off of his head and tossed it on his bed. As he was unwrapping his fists, a smirk crossed his lips.

Free at last, free at last, thank God Almighty, I'm free at last, he thought.

***

Cody lay in bed inside of the infirmary eating a fruit cup when he saw Tyson and a CO come through the door. His cousin resembled a young Mekhi Phifer. He had a close fade and a goatee that framed his mouth perfectly, compliments of the prison barber no doubt. He was wearing a white thermal, gray Dickies and black All Star Chuck Taylor Converse. He smiled from ear to ear approaching his relative's bed, boasting the prettiest set of white teeth and gap.

"What's up, baby boy?" Tyson slapped hands with Cody.

"What it is, relative?" he scraped the last of the diced peaches out of the cup and set the empty container down on his tray.

THESE SCANDALOUS STREETS

Tyson looked to the Correctional officer and said, "Yo', boss, you mind giving us a minute?" the burly, red faced guard made an about-face and left the two cousins to themselves. "I chopped it up with that nigga Grief a while ago." He informed his relative.

"For real? What blood say?" he sat up in bed.

"He lifted the bounty off your head, so you good."

"Yeah, at what cost?" he folded his arms across his chest, wrinkles forming on his forehead.

"Old head wants me to be his daughter's bodyguard. You know the singer, Treasure Gold?"

"Hell yeah, that bitch fine than a mothafucka. That's who I be thinking about when I be whacking off in our cell."

Tyson laughed and shook his head. "Anyway, it's a paying gig so I'll be all right to lay some cash on your books and shit."

"So how long does the gig last?"

"'Til your time is up."

"So all you gotta do is watch homegirl's back to get me square with this nigga?"

"Yeah."

"Sounds easy enough."

"I hope so."

"Who's springing you from out this piece, Uncle Henry?"

"Nah, my bro."

"That brazy mothafucka Moon? Tell'em I said what's bracking?"

"McGowan!" the CO's voice boomed from the door, letting him know it was time for his departure.

"Well, look, C. Let me get from up outta here for they change their mind and try to keep a nigga." Tyson slapped hands with Cody and gave him a long embrace. "I love you, nigga."

"I love you too, reli. I'll see you in a year." Cody said after they'd broken their embrace. He watched as his kin strolled out of the door with the CO following shortly behind.

***

Moon leaned his husky frame against his '87 Buick Regal, smoking a Newport. He checked his red G-Shock for the fifth time, tapping his foot on the ground as he impatiently waited for his little brother to exit the gates of Hell. He hadn't seen his sibling in four summers, so excitement was an understatement when it came to explaining how anxious he was to see him.

Buzzzzz!

The gates of the correctional facility opened and out waltz Tyson smiling from ear to ear, showcasing the small gap between his top row of teeth. You'd have thought he won the lottery the way he was cheesing. He dropped down to his knees and kissed the ground. Moon mashed his cigarette out under his sneaker and moved to greet his brother. The two men embraced. He then stepped back and gave him the once over.

"Damn, Blood, you done got big than a mothafucka, Ty." He commented on his slightly bulky frame.

"Pumping iron and eating, man," Tyson showed off his "18 arms.

"You ain't never too big to get cho ass knocked out, though." Moon shot back playfully throwing punches at his him. He bobbed, weaved, and threw some of his own.

THESE SCANDALOUS STREETS

"I'm home, baby, your baby brother is free!" Tyson yelled at the top of his lungs before embracing his brother again. "Damn, Zippa, this is your ride? I can't believe you still whipping this piece of shit. I thought Yvette would have died on you by now."

"Man, I'm not ever getting rid of my baby. This hooptie is like my bottom bitch, been witta nigga through my ups and downs, feel me?"

"Hey, if you like it I love it." Tyson replied.

Buzzzz!

The gate buzzing again drew Tyson and his sibling's attention to their rear. The barbed wire gate rolled back and Malakai came strolling out, a sack of his belongings slung over his shoulder. He stopped where he was and closed his eyes. A smile spread across his thick lips as he held a hand above his brows and surveyed his surroundings. He took his hand away and moved his head from left to right, allowing the blazing sapphire in the sky's warm rays to bath over his head and neck. It felt good to be free, damn good. When he locked eyes with Tyson he threw his head back like *What's up, my nigga?* He returned the gesture with a smile.

"Let me get up with this nigga 'fore we leave." Tyson tapped his brother before starting in Malakai's direction. Just as he was approaching a black on black Escalade on some pretty ass chrome thangs was driving up to the penitentiary. The sun shining on it caused its chrome grill, door handles and "24 rims to gleam. "Is that cho people?" he asked the man that had saved his ass, glancing at the SUV and throwing a thumb over his shoulder.

"Yeah." Malakai nodded, outstretching his hand.

Tyson slapped hands with him and embraced him, patting him on his back.

THESE SCANDALOUS STREETS

"Thanks, fam, I really mean that," he spoke with dead serious eyes.

"Don't mention it," he replied like it was nothing.

"Nah, you saved my life. If there's anything I can do for you, you just let me know."

Malakai nodded. "Alright, I may call your marker one day."

"Fa sho'. You know what chu gon' do now that chu free?"

"Hmmph," he smiled. It was from this that Tyson knew that he was getting back on his bullshit, selling drugs. And he couldn't blame him either. He was a convicted felon now and weren't too many businesses willing to hire a nigga with a black eye on his record. Many ex-cons didn't have a choice once they were released but to go back to getting it how they lived.

"I ain't mad at cha family. Niggaz gotta eat, right?"

"Sho' ya right." He threw a finger up at the Escalade for the driver to give him a minute. "What about chu, my nigga? What chu coming home to?"

"I'ma be your people's bodyguard."

"Who?" a line indented his forehead.

"Treasure Gold." He smiled.

"Really? How'd that happen?"

Treasure and Blessyn were on the same label, Big Willie records. They were the biggest stars on it. Every now and again Malakai and his crew would hit the clubs with them when they went to perform. They'd sit up in VIP popping bottles, smoking, and picking up any groupies that Blessyn passed up on. Everyone at Big Willie was really familiar with the superstar rapper and his niggaz. They treated him like he was family. And why wouldn't they when his brother was their biggest act and top grosser. They wanted to stay in his good graces.

"The old man saw what I could do with these—" he held up his fists. "—and gave me a gig."

"Simple as that, huh?"

"Yep. It's a catch to it though."

"What's that?"

Tyson gave him a quick rundown on him and the OG's agreement.

"I knew it was something to him not wetting up ya shirt and mine." He shook his head pitifully.

"I take it you're the reason why I'm walking out this bitch instead of being carried out, huh?" he said as he threw his hand toward the prison behind him.

Malakai and Grief hadn't gotten along ever since he gave one of his people that work over a card game. When he made the con that was being ran on him he politely excused himself. He played it cool for an entire week until he caught him slipping one day coming out of the shower room. With the stealth of a panther, he crept up on him from behind, pulled him back by his hair, and stabbed him in his voice box, twisting it around. It was from that incident that the stud would forever speak with a whisper which was how he'd garnered his nickname, Whispers.

"Yeah, I talked him into getting you cut loose."

"Good looking out, homeboy."

"I'm just returning the love."

"No doubt."

"Yo', Ty." Moon called out, making his brother turn around. "Let's get up; it's hot as fuck out here." He wiped his sweaty forehead with the lower inside of his shirt.

"Alright." Tyson turned back around to Malakai. "Let me get up outta here, fam."

THESE SCANDALOUS STREETS

"I'm sure we'll run into one another again, I fucks with cha boy Showtime."

"You gotta number I can reach chu at?"

"Yeah, I can slide you my grandmomma's until I get a cell. You gotta pen?"

"I can record it." He tapped his temple. Once he received the telephone number, he dapped up the hustler and they made their departure.

Tyson was on his way home.

THESE SCANDALOUS STREETS

Chapter Four

Malakai watched the Regal until it was out of sight before starting towards the black beauty that was his ride home. His right and left hands, Crazy and Bizeal, hopped out of the ebony beast, smiles plastered across their faces. Approaching them his face also broadened with a smile. He hadn't seen his niggaz in quite some time. Being that they were convicted felons like himself, they couldn't come see him so he kept in contact through a contraband cell phone he'd purchased on lock.

A jovially expression accented Crazy's face when his nigga approached. He snatched the toothpick from between his lips for a proper greeting.

"What's up, boy?"

Malakai slapped hands with the shortest one out of his crew and pulled him in for a gangsta hug. When he pulled back he took a good look at him. He'd traded in his cornrows for a close fade and his once skinny frame was now defined by some muscle. He was the youngest out of their crew and probably the most dangerous, as he was willing to go above and beyond to get his point across. That's why they'd christened him with the name Crazy.

"Ain't shit, I'm glad to see yo' mothafucking ass though, it's been a minute." Crazy replied, looking his homeboy over. "Man, yo' ass is big as a brick shit house, fuck you been lifting in there, dump trucks?"

"Bitch…niggaz." Malakai made each of his pecks jump and smirked.

"I heard that." He nodded.

They slapped hands and hugged again.

THESE SCANDALOUS STREETS

"Welcome home, my nigga." Bizeal greeted him with his meaty hand. They slapped palms and embraced with a brotherly hug. It had been eight long years and he looked almost the same as he'd left him. He still rocked a gold grill but his light brown dreads had grown out and lay sprawled across his shoulders. Not to mention the extra thirty pounds he'd picked up. He was more so husky than fat.

"Glad to be back." His eyes shot to the black velvet sack in his hand and his brows wrinkled.

"Is that what I think it is?" he said while pointing to the sack which looked to be holding some pretty heavy contents.

"Yep," Bizeal replied and passed it to him.

Malakai sat the sack on the hood of the Escalade and drew it open by its drawstrings. When the sun's rays casted against what was inside a rainbow casted upon his face and he smiled, showcasing all thirty two of his teeth. He was in awe at the jewelry that lay inside. Looking to Bizeal he asked, "You got everything all cleaned up for me, Zeal?"

"Yeah, I got that outta the way before we dipped down here to get chu." He stood beside his friend as he fished through the contents of the sack.

The first two pieces of jewelry he put on was a chunky ass gold pinky ring flooded with diamonds. That bitch sparkled as soon as the light hit it. He slid it onto his pinky finger and kissed it like it was a good luck charm. Next, he came out with a presidential gold Rolex which he slipped on the same hand as his ring. Then there was his most prized possession. A Cuban link chain that held onto a medallion that was an icy Jesus piece. Malakai held it up like it was the bronze meadow at The Olympics, eyeing it with admiration before looping it over his head. He threw open the front passenger side door and planted his ass in the seat, flipping down the sun visor. Smiling, he gave himself the once over

THESE SCANDALOUS STREETS

marveling his appearance in the jewels. Flipping the sun visor shut, he closed his eyes and reflected on the night he was blessed with them. They were gifts from his deceased brother.

"Momma, what are you doin'?" Blessyn shouted, with his palms on both sides of his forehead, wrinkling the skin.

Mrs. Williams stood over the opened commode, wringing out a gym sock over it. Packets of heroin labeled Pandemonium hit the toilet water floating around. Without hesitation, she smacked the commode's lid down and flushed the drugs down.

"What the hell," Blessyn darted over to the commode and flipped the lid open. Plunging his hands into the water, he was able to snatch up a couple of packets before they were washed away. Holding up the packets to the light he saw that the water had ruined what was inside. "Aww, man! You know how much money you just flushed down the fucking toilet?"

Smack!

Her meaty palm went across his face and snapped it to the right, silencing him. He slowly turned his head back around to her, humbled. His cheek was stinging with redness.

"You mind your mouth in my home!" She stared up at him with glassy eyes on the brink of tears, pointing her finger in his face.

"Yes, ma'am," He conceded feeling the stinging in his cheek from her assault. Right there on the spot he reverted back to the eight year old boy she'd raised by her lonesome.

"I didn't raise you to be no drug dealer, out here pushing poison in the streets to ya own kind? Have you no shame?"

THESE SCANDALOUS STREETS

Blessyn's eyes shifted up to the bathroom door where he found a fifteen year old Malakai peering inside.

"Young man," she slammed her fist on the bathroom sink vibrating the medicine cabinet mirror. Her oldest grandson's eyes shifted to hers. "You hear me talking to you?"

"I hear you momma, but I'm out here doin' what I gotta do to take care of us, this family." He jabbed his finger into the bathroom sink getting his point across. "I'm the..."

"Watch yo' tone and yo' delivery now." Her eyes widened and she angled her head.

He took a deep breath and started over. "I'm the man of this family. Therefore, I'm the protector and the provider. I'm just doin' how my father taught me."

She pulled a stack of bills out of her house coat and shook it at him. "With this dirty money!"

"That dirty money is keepin' the lights on and food on the table."

"Well, not anymore," she held the money at both ends and ripped it up into shreds, allowing the pieces to fall to the floor.

"What the hell, ma!" his eyes bulged and he clutched his heart. He couldn't believe she'd just ripped up two thousand dollars. He scrambled at her feet trying to salvage whatever bills he could possibly tape back together. There wasn't anything worth having though.

"You brought drugs into my home, around your brother..." She threw a hand over her shoulder.

"Fffff." He bit down on his bottom lip trying not to say Fuck and disrespect his grandma. There wasn't a hundred dollar bill on the floor worth keeping. Slowly, he got upon his feet, getting up with his palm on his knee.

THESE SCANDALOUS STREETS

"I want you out of my house…" a shock expression swept over his face. He couldn't believe what he was hearing.

"But momma…"

"Tonight!" As soon as the words left her lips, the tears streamed down her chubby, black moled cheeks.

"Can I getta few nights, ma? Gimmie three days." He threw up three fingers. "Three days and I'll be outta here."

"God knows I love you and yo' brother with all that I am…" Her lips quivered and she laid her hands over her heart. "I did all that I could to raise you right, but I guess I failed you." His eyes misted with tears which rimmed his eyelids and threatened to spill. "I…I…I cannot allow you inside of my home not one more night…you have to leave."

When Blessyn saw his brother was still watching at the door he hurriedly blinked back his tears. Although he saw tears accumulating in his sibling's eyes too it didn't matter. See, he wanted to be the epitome of strength. He was The Man of the family. And to allow those tears to manifest would forever tarnish his brother's image of him, or so he thought.

"Alright, momma, if you want me gon' then I'm gon'." He moved to leave the bathroom and Malakai sprinted off down the hallway. As soon as Blessyn crossed the threshold out of the bathroom his grandmother closed the door behind him. It clicked shut. He could hear her muffled sobs resonating at his rear as he made his way down the corridor. Once he entered him and his brother bedroom. He found him lying back in his twin bed, headphones on as he flipped through a Source magazine pretending not to even notice him. They both knew that he was fronting though, but he didn't care enough to address it.

THESE SCANDALOUS STREETS

Over the top of his magazine Malakai watched him grab a duffle bag and begin stuffing it with underwear and socks. Afterwards he grabbed his clothes from inside of the closet and threw them on top of the bed. Next, he grabbed his .380 from underneath the mattress along with several packets of heroin which he dumped into the bag.

Malakai snatched off the headphones and flung the magazine aside, sitting up on the bed.

"Where you going?" *Creases dipped on his forehead.*

"Momma kickin' me out, you heard her." *He shuffled through the CDs on the shelf trying to find which ones were his.*

"You want me to talk to her? I could see if she'd let chu stay."

"Nah." *He shook his head no.* "I'm nineteen years old. It's time I left the nest anyway."

"What about me? I wanna go with you." *he rose from the bed.*

This made Blessyn stop and turn around to him. "You can't."

"Why? And don't tell me I'm too young either, I'm fifteen."

" I know that, you a grown ass man." *He cracked a slight smile, looking up at him as he shoved the CDs into his bag. Seeing that his younger brother was getting angry, he addressed the situation more delicately.* "Look, you can't come with me. Momma's gonna need somebody here to look after her and the house. We live in the Nickerson's shit ain't safe here. She's gon' need someone to protect her."

"Yeah, well, how am I 'pose to do that with no gun? My fists ain't gon' do too much against bullets."

"True dat." *He nodded his agreement, picking up his .380 and waving him over. Once he came he gave him the*

THESE SCANDALOUS STREETS

gun. As soon as that cold metal met with his palms he felt a surge in power and height. Malakai closed one eye and aimed the weapon around the room. "Humph." Blessyn smirked. Digging inside of his duffle bag he pulled out two scratched up magazines for the gun and passed them to his brother.

"You really gonna let me have this?" he referred to the gun.

"Yep." He nodded. "You're gon' need something to hold the house down being that you're the man of it and all. Just don't make me regret it. I'm sure you won't though. You aren't like the rest of these lil' ass niggaz that's running around in these projects, you smart."

"Thanks, but won't chu need a piece since you're gonna be out in the streets?"

"I stay witta thang or two, bro bro. Here," he pulled out a fat knot and passed him ten one hundred dollar bills. When Malakai's hand grasped the money his eyes went big and he looked at it like Wow. That was the most paper he'd ever had in his hands so it was a big deal to him. "That's all you."

Malakai stuffed the money into his pocket and tucked the .380 and the magazines underneath his mattress. When he turned around his brother was cramming a pen and notepad inside of his duffle bag. Next, he was stepping into the dresser mirror and tying a red bandana around his dome Tupac style.

"Where you gonna go?" Malakai worried, lines coming across his forehead.

"I'ma crash at that nigga TyBudd house, he's gotta studio up in that bitch." He turned around from the dresser, folding his arms across the chest. "We're gonna go to work on my demo. He's gotta few connects and we're gonna see about shopping it around. Hopefully I'll land a deal. Until

THESE SCANDALOUS STREETS

then I'ma be out in these streets trappin' like its finna go outta style." He gave his younger sibling the cold, hard truth. They were always up front with one another no matter what.

Malakai nodded his understanding, feeling where his brother was coming from. He looked up to him and respected him. Blessyn was bigger than the president to him. He held onto his every word and tailored himself after him. The youngster wanted to be exactly like him. Like Kanye West said My Big Brother.

"Don't worry, man, yo' big bruh gon' be alright," he held up his Kansas City Chiefs jersey showcasing his Kevlar bulletproof vest. He knocked on it and let it fall back down over it. His brother smiled. Blessyn was heavy in the streets so death was right around the corner. Shit, he'd shot niggas and he'd been shot. It was the survival of the fittest inside of The Concrete Jungle so he had to show fools he was willing to die and kill for his. "See, I'm straight."

"I see. You still gonna get me that chain I wanted for my birthday?"

Blessyn bowed his head and massaged his chin as he thought on it. When he looked up to his brother he was wearing a hopeful grin on his lips. "I do you one betta. Come here," he hung his head and undid his gold Cuban link chain with the Jesus piece dangling from the end of it. The medallion was sparkling in diamonds. He held it pinched between his fingers and thumbs awaiting his brother. Once Malakai turned his back to him, he slipped the jewelry around his neck and snapped it closed. Afterwards, he pulled off his huge diamond pinky ring and slid it onto his sibling's pinky finger. Right after, he was slipping his presidential Rolex around his wrist. His brother looked up at him like he couldn't believe that he was giving all of these

THESE SCANDALOUS STREETS

things to him. He dared not to mention it for fear of him coming to his senses and taking everything back. Blessyn ushered him over to the dresser mirror and stood beside him, with his hand on his shoulder. He cracked a smile seeing how happy his sibling was with his gifts. The little nigga held the chain pinched between his fingers and thumbs. He looked to the twinkling jewelry and back up to the mirror. "You like it?"

"Like it? This mothafucka hard." He couldn't keep his eyes off of the chain, watch, and pinky ring adorning him. The youngster stood in the mirror smiling like he was waiting to have his picture taken. "You gon' let me have this for real?"

"Yeah, why not? You my lil' nigga." He grabbed his duffle bag and approached his brother, dapping him up. "I'm outta here, fam. You got the number to my cell, bang my line if you need me."

He made for the door but his brother calling him back made him turn around, raising an eyebrow. Suddenly, little brother collided with big brother, wrapping his arms around him lovingly. He cracked a smile and threw his free arm around him.

"I love you, man."

"I love you, too, Mal."

Reminiscing back to that night caused Malakai's eyes to rim with tears. He was still locked up when he got the word through a kite that his brother had been murdered. The news left him devastated. A death hadn't left him with such a void in his life since the ones of his parents, who'd died in an automobile accident on the 405 freeway. Malakai felt like he was suffocating and a hot sword was piercing his heart. As soon as he was released from his house for chow he kicked off a prison yard riot that left fourteen wounded and another

THESE SCANDALOUS STREETS

eight dead. He knew that he was dead ass wrong but he didn't give a mad ass fuck, he needed a vice to unleash that hurt and turmoil that had built up inside of him.

"You straight, my nigga?" Bizeal questioned with concern from behind the wheel of the behemoth, looking from the windshield to his homeboy.

"Yeah, I'm good." Malakai blinked back the wetness in his eyes and wiped them with a jeweled hand, sniffling. "I got something in my eye." He turned his head out of the window and watched the streets pass him by rapidly. Warmth settled into his eyes and tears came spilling down his cheeks. He'd fell victim yet again to the memories of his sibling. "I miss you bro bro, I miss you so fucking much, man." He spoke under his breath, hoping that somehow and some way that his kin was listening.

Malakai promised himself that once he touched down that he was going to rebuild his empire and catch up with whomever it was that gave his brother the business.

***

Treasure stood in the mirror of the bathroom conjoined to her bedroom brushing her teeth. Once she was done, she rinsed out her mouth and pulled her hair back in a ponytail, studying her reflection. She couldn't help but think of the lyrics to that old Drake song since she was in the same digs as the girl he was talking about.

Sweatpants, hair tied, chillin' with no makeup on/ That's when you're the prettiest I hope that you don't take it wrong.

Treasure grimaced as she showcased her teeth, turning her head from side to side. All thirty two teeth were white, looking like flawless pearls. After putting up the Scope mouthwash and her toothbrush, she flicked the light-switch off on her way out of the bathroom. Crossing the threshold onto the thick mink carpet of her bedroom, she threw her manicured feet into a pair of house slippers. She turned to head out of the door to fix herself some breakfast when something caught her eye. Her face scrunched up and she turned around, eyes finding the portrait of her and Blessyn on the nightstand. A smirk accented her face as she picked it up, sliding her French tip nails down it. She remembered that night like it was yesterday, although it was almost seven years ago.

Knock! Knock! Knock! Knock!

The sudden rapping at the door startled her and she almost dropped the portrait.

"Who is it?" she called out.

"'Sup, Treas? You decent in there, baby girl?" Showtime spoke from the other side of the door.

"Yeah, gimmie a sec." she sat the portrait back down on the dresser and opened the door. She stepped aside and allowed the men to enter. Showtime pecked her on the cheek and plopped down on the bed.

"You doing alright?" he asked her, referring to what occurred at the Garden before crossing his legs.

"Yeah, I'm okay." She sat down on her bed.

"You speak to your old man?"

"Yeah, a couple of nights ago."

Showtime and Keith exchanged knowing glances. Treasure picked right up on it, brows furrowing.

"Come on now. You know I know better than that," she said lighting a cigarette and tossing the lighter back on the nightstand. She lay back against the headboard and blew smoke into the air.

THESE SCANDALOUS STREETS

"I don't know how he found out, but he already knew. He said that he was going to see about changing some things that would insure my safety from now on."

"It leaked," Showtime told Keith of the incident back at the Garden. "You think it was somebody on the team?"

"I wouldn't be surprised. Them niggaz are as chatty as a couple of old broads at a card game," Keith said from where he stood in the bedroom.

"What's up?"

"I gotta call from your father the other day. He wanted to let me know that he was sending someone here for you; your own personal bodyguard."

"After what just happened I don't think that's a bad idea."

"Just fuck me, huh?" Keith retorted with a frown.

"Awww, you know I wuv you, Keefe Poo," Treasure spoke to him like she was a toddler, pinching his cheek. "But you're only one man, and one man can only do so much." She looked to Showtime. "Who's the guy?"

"Some cat from Los Angeles. He's off the Eastside. Some area called The Low Bottoms."

"Is he any good?"

"From what I hear, yes." The H.N.I.C at Big Willie records rose from the bed. "Well, that's it. I was just giving you the heads up. He'll be here tomorrow. Come on, Keith."

"Wait a minute, Show." She called after him just before he went through the door.

He turned around to her. "'Sup?"

"What's this guy's name?"

"Tyson."

THESE SCANDALOUS STREETS

Chapter Five

The Stylistics softly flowed from the speakers of Moon's Regal as he drove down the freeway back to the hood. Tyson stuck his head out of the window and closed his eyes. He smiled as the fresh, cool air washed over his face and head.

Tyson pulled his head back inside and lit up a cigarette. He took a pull and then blew smoke, letting it be vacuumed out by the cracked window.

"So, what's up, Zippa? What're you up to now? Fill me in."

"You know me, same old same old," Moon said, looking from the windshield to his brother occasionally. "You know it's always been the way of the gun for me. I stay with that mask and that bag, every night is Halloween. How you think your commissary stayed so fat? I got myself a new ride, too. BMW 745. This is just my company car, if you know what I mean." He smiled and winked.

"So, you're doing all right for yourself, huh?"

"Yeah, I'm doing okay, I gotta lil' spot too, out there in Glendale. You can use the address there for your parole, if you want."

"Cool. What up with the old crew?"

"After Gangsta got locked up, Booby picked up right where he left off."

"For real?"

"Yep, the homie caking off too, he's doing the damn thang," Moon said seriously. "I'm telling you how Gangsta had it going, ain't shit compared to how Booby laying it down now. My nigga a hood billionaire, he got most of the homies working for him. Ridah Man, Debo, Woo, Big Head, Panic, Gouch."

THESE SCANDALOUS STREETS

"Blood tried to put me on, too. But chu know me, I get mine the ski-mask way. That crack money might be for sho'money but its slow money. I can't see myself grinding in somebody's spot for their trap all day and night. Uh uh, I'd rather let some other fool do all of the hard work, while I plot on how to take all his shit, feel me?"

"True that." Tyson nodded and took a pull from the cigarette.

"So, what're your plans, Zippa?" Moon switched subjects. "I gotta couple licks lined up, or are you squaring up?"

"I made a couple connects in prison and this cat's peoples are hooking me up with this gig, so I'ma work that."

"Bool, what's up with our lil' reli?"

"Who, Cody? He's straight. He told me to tell you, 'What's bracking?'"

"Yeah, I'm 'pose to lay some ends on his books and shit. I'ma do that after I finish taking you shopping." He took in his attire. His thermal was extra snug thanks to the muscle he'd packed on and his Dickies were damn near flooding.

"Good looking out. A nigga could use some new threads." He gave himself the once over.

"Don't mention it; I gotta look out for my baby bruh."

Moon and Tyson went to every clothing store they could think of. Having been down for four years Tyson was ignorant to the latest fashions, so he put him on to what was in. By the time they were finished shopping the trunk of the Regal and the backseat were loaded with shopping bags. It was after four o'clock p.m. in the evening when they finally made it to their father's house.

"Good looking on the gear and shit, bro."

"It ain't 'bout nothing." He waved him off. "Let's put this stuff up and holler at pop."

THESE SCANDALOUS STREETS

After putting up his underwear and hanging up his clothes, Tyson straightened up his bedroom and headed to the backyard. When he and his brother made it to the backyard their father had just finished a set and sat the barbell on the hooks of the weight bench. He sat up panting and rested his gloved hands on his thighs. His dark skin glistened under the sun having been covered in beads of sweat. The old man grabbed a white towel and wiped his face and bare chest down.

"Your youngest is here, pop." Moon patted his brother on the shoulder.

When Henry McGowan saw his youngest boy, his lips formed a toothy smile. Father and son embraced, hugging each other lovingly.

Henry had served in the Vietnam War and had earned every accolade you could possibly imagine. After being honorably discharged he returned home to work as a construction worker. He was forced to be a single dad once Tyson and Moon's mother left him for another man. It was tough but he did the best he could. He brought discipline and guidance into his sons lives, but in the end it wasn't enough to sway them from the call of the streets.

"Damn, it's good to see you, boy." Henry pecked his second born on the cheek and held him at arm's length, grinning. "You look good."

"You look good too, pop." Tyson returned the compliment. "What chu got some "16 arms? You're built like Michael Jai White."

"Fuck is Michael Jai White?" he frowned.

"Homeboy that starred in the Blood and Bone movie."

"Oh, these are "17, son." He corrected him as he pumped the barbell up and down, hairy chest swelling and deflating. "So when are you due back in prison?"

THESE SCANDALOUS STREETS

"I'm not ever going back, pop." He claimed seriously.

"Yeah, that's what that knucklehead over there told me." Henry grimaced referring to Moon.

"Nah, I'm serious. The pen ain't for me."

"What's your plans?"

"I gotta gig, starts tomorrow evening."

"Doing what?" Tyson filled his brother and father in on the armed bodyguard job with Big Willie records. Only he left out the circumstances of why he was forced to take the gig. "That's good, son. You just be careful. There's plenty crazies out here running around behind these celebrities."

"I know, pop."

Tyson sat talking with his brother and father for the duration of the day. They ate dinner and watched old James Cagney movies. *White Heat* was one of his favorite films. Afterwards, he showered and got dressed for his rendezvous with Monique. He retrieved the car keys from his sibling and headed out the door. He went to cross the street to his brother's ride and a black Mercedes Benz pulled into his path. He went to draw his head bussa and the vehicle's back window rolled down, revealing a very familiar face inside.

"What's happening, Blood?" A brown skinned man behind Aviator shades asked, clapping his hands and laughing. He seemed to be really happy to see him.

"What's up, my nigga?" Tyson embraced Booby Loco when he stepped from the backseat.

"When you get out, Blood?" Booby inquired.

"This morning, I see the homies done came up while I was gone." He held his old friend's platinum medallion in his hand. The piece was of the earth and flooded with green and blue diamonds. Its outside was surrounded by the words *The World Is Mine* which had black diamonds in every letter. The piece belonged to the biggest link around the young

THESE SCANDALOUS STREETS

kingpin's neck. The second link was smaller and held a diamond crucifix that twinkled under the illumination of the light post.

Booby shrugged his shoulders. "I'm doing all right." He spoke modestly.

"My nigga, you doing more than *all right*," he gave him the once over. He was fitted in a navy blue L.A New Era fitted cap, a navy blue blazer over a pinstriped buttoned-down, Levi's 501 jeans and white on white Air Force Ones.

"Wish I would have known you were getting out, though. I would have put a lil' something together for you." He rubbed his jeweled, manicured hands together.

"It's cool, I'm headed to a lil' shindig of my own." He held up a bottle of Hennessy. "Where my nigga Gucci at?"

"He's somewhere in these streets, fam. You know my brother. He doesn't like anyone keeping tabs on him."

"So, what's up? You need a job, or something? You know I could always use someone with your skills on the team."

"Nah, thanks but no thanks. I gotta gig. It starts tomorrow, as a matter of fact. Besides, you know that line of work ain't never been my thang."

"I Griff you, but let me at least bless you," Booby pulled a wad of $100 dollar bills from his pocket. He peeled off twenty of them and held them out for Tyson to take.

"I can't accept that, Booby, man." He held up his hands like a gun was pulled on him.

"Nigga, if you don't take this money, I'ma take it as an insult and we're gonna be fighting out here," he said through clenched jaws, playfully.

Tyson chuckled and took the money. "Thanks."

THESE SCANDALOUS STREETS

"You know how we do." When he went to stick the money back into his pocket, Tyson noticed the gun bulging beneath his shirt.

It's a good thing to stay strapped, especially with all of the jewels this nigga got on. The homie's looking like a Jack Boy's wet dream out here.

"Pavy, we're gonna be late for the movie." A dime piece stuck her head out of the backseat. She was of a rose gold complexion. She had greenish blue eyes that looked like two globes of the earth, full lips, and long curly sandy brown hair. Baby had a face and body that belonged on the pages of Double XL's Eye Candy.

"Oh, hi." The beauty smiled and waved to Tyson.

He smiled and waved back, remembering her face from the picture Booby sent him in prison. "How are you doing? I'm Tyson."

"Vayda," she introduced herself. "I've heard so much about you. It's nice to meet you."

"Same here," he replied, then turned to Booby. "Well, look, my nigga. I'ma gon' and get outta here." He slapped hands with his homeboy.

"Alright, if you change your mind about the job, hit me up." The young kingpin yelled to Tyson as he jogged across the street. Tyson threw up their hood before hopping into the Regal and pulling off.

***

When Tyson rolled up to Monique's place she was already waiting outside on the curb. She hopped in and he pulled off, laughing to himself. He figured a John does the same thing with a whore on the stroll. He pulls up, they negotiate a price, she hops in and he drives away. Suckers like that paid for pussy but not him. The only thing he was giving old girl was hard dick and conversation.

"What are you laughing at?" Monique asked. She was a redbone with a Coca Cola bottle shape. Her hair was flat-ironed and highlighted by burgundy streaks. Her dimples were pierced with diamond studs.

"Nothing, some shit that happened earlier."

"I missed him." she said with a seductive look, licking her big lip glossed lips.

"Who?" Tyson's forehead wrinkled.

"Him," She grabbed the bulge in his jeans.

"Why don't you show him how much you missed *him*?" With that said, she unzipped his jeans, freeing his thick, veined penis from its confiment. She worked his anaconda until it rose to attention, the head of it swollen. Her warm, salivating mouth took in his full length as she deep throated him. Waves of pleasure gyrated throughout his southern region.

"Mmmmm." His eyes flickered as he groaned and mashed the peddle giving the vehicle more gas. The Regal sped up a notch and he damn near collided into oncoming traffic. "Oh, fuck!" he bellowed, pressing one hand against the ceiling, his hand imprinting the fabric.

Feeling his throbbing dickhead in the back of her throat, Monique brought her head up and wiped her mouth on the sleeve of her jean jacket. Thereafter, she removed a small black box of Trojan magnums from a brown paper bag. She opened the box and removed a golden foil wrapped lubricated condom. She tore open the wrapper and used her mouth to put the rubber on him, rolling it down to the stubble of his mound. Next, she pulled up her jean skirt and pulled her black thong to the side, exposing her shaved vagina. She lined her sex up with his, and slowly lowered herself onto his

THESE SCANDALOUS STREETS

lap. Monique gasped, feeling Tyson's girth fill the void between her sugar walls.

"Ssssss, damn, nigga," she hissed, eyes rolling to their whites as she leaned her head back. She worked her hips like a belly dancer. The danger of wrecking only heightened the sexual experience. Tyson's left eye squinted and his mouth fell open. She rode him like a cowgirl, her hips moving like the waves of the ocean.

Tyson snuck a peek at the speedometer; he was doing sixty running through red lights and stop signs. He looked to the digital clock in the stereo, twelve minutes had passed since they'd left Monique's grandmother's house. Another three minutes went by before the hooptie screeched to a stop at a red light and he exploded inside of her, filling the latex. He held the brake pedal down and lay back in the seat, panting.

"Haa! Haa! Haa! Haa!"

She continued to work his half erect love muscle until she screamed and creamed. Her lather soiled part of his sweatshirt and jeans. She smiled, brushed a strand of hair behind her ear and kissed him.

Back at the motel they consumed the entire bottle of Hennessy and smoked two blunts. They took half of a blue Transformer each and went at it for two more rounds. Tyson awoke to catch the sun peeking over the horizon. He woke Monique up so they could shower and get dressed. When he dropped her off at home she kissed him goodbye. She was a woman who knew how to please a man in every way. Her only problem was she was a hood rat. If it wasn't for that he would have wifed her.

THESE SCANDALOUS STREETS

Chapter Six
The next day

"Mr. Sams, my grandson has been dead for the past five years now. And his killer has yet to be brought to justice. I wanna know what measures are being taken to arrest the man that murdered him," Mrs. Williams said angrily, stomping her cane into the floor. She was a seventy five year old woman who wore her hair in a gray afro. She wore a pearl necklace and a P-coat over a purple pants suit and flats.

Chief Sams stopped filling out the paperwork that lay before him on the desk top. He dropped his pen on the document and lay back in the executive chair, clearing his throat with a fist to his mouth.

"Mrs. Williams, I assure you that we're doing everything we possibly can to find your grandson's killer. Unfortunately, we do have other cases that we're handling also, so we can't just focus on his alone," Chief Sams informed her. He was a man fifty six years in age who rocked a bald head that shined like polished pattern leather shoes. He was light skinned with a sprinkle of freckles over his cheeks and nose.

"I already told you, Mr. Sams, it was the fella that owned the label he was signed under. Now, I don't know if the son of a bitch pulled the trigger himself, but I do know he had something to do with it. I'm telling you I can feel it every time I'm around him. He has a bad aura surrounding him."

"Ma'am, you're being absurd, we can't just go making arrests every time a victim's relative makes an assumption."

"Well, can't you at least bring him in for questioning?"

He looked away and blew hot air before turning back around to her. "Good afternoon, Mrs. Williams."

He went back to scribbling something down on a document.

THESE SCANDALOUS STREETS

Mrs. Williams stared at Chief Sams for a time. She clenched and unclenched her jaws and her nose flared. The old lady was so hot that you could fry a couple of strips of bacon on her forehead. Tilting her head, she closed her eyes for a moment and swallowed her steam. It took all of the self-control that she could muster not to snatch her nickel plated .32 from out of her coat and put some hot shit in his face. With a heavy head and an even heavier heart she turned and walked out of the office, slamming the door shut so hard that it rattled the portraits and awards on the wall.

Mrs. Williams came out of the precinct and leaned against the doorway. She wiped the tears that stained her face with her coat's sleeve before heading down the steps, sniffling. Walking towards her car she passed a huge monument of her grandson sprayed painted on the side of a liquor store. It was Blessyn rapping to an audience. He was bare chest and beads of sweat covered him, a gold necklace which held to a .357 Magnum revolver charm dangled from his neck. Below him was his birth and death date. The streets loved Mrs. Williams' grandson just as much as she did. But while the streets went on with their lives after his death she would not rest until her grandson's killer was brought to justice.

The night

Malakai had spent the majority of the day getting reacquainted with his niggas and his grandmother. After spending time with the woman that raised him, the homies took him to M & M's off of King and Crenshaw Boulevard where they all ate heartily. The men chopped it up amongst each other and brought their homeboy up to speed on the dealings in the streets. Afterwards, the fellas took him

THESE SCANDALOUS STREETS

shopping. He tore the mothafucking mall up and purchased the new iPhone 6. Now here they were dropping him off at his girl's apartment out in Compton.

"Alright, I'll get up with chu niggaz tomorrow." Malakai dapped up his homeboys and grabbed his shopping mall bags, climbing out of the black beauty.

"I'll bang yo' line in the AM." Bizeal hollered out of the driver side window as his homie rounded the truck.

Malakai gave him a nod while en route to the apartment complex. He carried his bags in one hand while the other worked the touch screen of his cell phone. When he found *Momma* in his list of contacts, he pressed it and brought it to his ear.

Honk! Honk!

Bizeal blew the horn twice before driving off and his man looked over his shoulder, throwing up a hand. He then turned his attention back to the conversation at hand.

"Ma, I was thinking you and I should go to church this Sunday. No, I'm not coming down with a fever, is it something wrong with me wanting to spend the day with my favorite girl?" He laughed hearing her reaction. She acted as if she couldn't believe him. "Yes, ma'am, I'm as serious as cancer. I'm going to pay my respects to The Man Upstairs with chu. I even bought myself a lil' suit and sh…I mean, stuff. Alright, I'll see you then, beautiful." He ended the call and shot his boo a text to let her know that he was on his way up. Right after he was stashing his cell inside of his pocket.

Malakai entered the complex through the black iron-gate without a hitch since the lock was busted. Jogging up the steps he spotted a baby in a shitty pamper sagging almost to the floor wandering around with a naked Barbie doll. A frown found its self upon his face as he looked around wondering where her parents were. Looking further ahead he

THESE SCANDALOUS STREETS

saw a unit's door cracked open. He scooped the baby into his arms and started for the unit.

"What chu doing out here, lil' momma?" He asked, bouncing her up and down on his arm. "One of these random ass niggas could have snatched you up and ran off." He pecked the cute baby on her saggy cheek and smirked. Malakai stuck his head inside of the apartment unit to find it littered with dope fiends that resembled reanimated corpses. They were either shooting up, preparing to, or in a deep nod. One dope fiend leaned further back than Neo did when he dodged that bullet in the Matrix. Malakai couldn't believe his equilibrium. He also couldn't fathom how disgusting the living quarters were. The walls were filthy. And a combination of dry blood, body fluids, and dirt had changed the carpet from cream to copper brown. The stench inside was overwhelming. It was feces coupled with urine. He gagged a bit, but managed to keep down his lunch.

Malakai gently pushed the baby inside and quietly closed the door shut before heading down the hall. He knocked on the door of the unit his girl stayed in. He heard someone shuffling around inside and then the locks being undid. The door pulled open to a chocolate beauty. Her tall stature married with her thickness gave her the appearance of an African warrior princess. Her hair was wrapped up in a scarf and a Kimono hugged her curvy frame. She shrieked; happy to see her man.

"Baybyeeee!" She leapt into his arms and wrapped her arms around his neck, covering his face with kisses as he carried her inside.

"Well, somebody's happy to see me." Malakai smiled, kicking the door closed behind him as he crossed the threshold into the apartment, carrying his wifey.

THESE SCANDALOUS STREETS

Fifteen minutes later

Malakai stood before the spray of the shower nozzle letting the hot water wash over his shaved head and toned abs. He'd taken a shower before he was released, but he wanted to cleanse the stench of being incarcerated from him. Besides, the five minute showers in prison paled in comparison to the long ones you could take at home. Hearing the glass sliding door of the bathtub come open, he looked over his shoulder to find Dakeemia wearing nothing but a smile. She slid the door closed behind her as she stepped inside, one manicured foot at a time. The chocolate goddess lathered up a washcloth with Dove body wash and proceeded to wash every inch of his muscular form. Once she was done he returned the favor and they stood under the spray of the hot liquid, passionately kissing as the water rinsed the soap suds from their bodies.

Malakai scooped Dakeemia up into his arms with ease and carried her off to the bedroom, dripping wet as he went along. He laid her across the bed and parted her thighs exposing her pretty shaved pussy. Next, he stuck his tongue between the lips below her waist; French kissed them like they were the ones on her face. "Haaa!" She gasped and pulled the sheets, it had been eight years since she felt a man. The beauty gave him the key to her heart as well as the one to her sex before he went in. So her pearl hadn't been pleasured since his iron vacation. "Ooooh, sweet, Jesus!" Dakeemia cried out, eyes squeezed shut and satisfaction smeared across her face. His sucking and murmuring filled her ears as he devoured her treasure. She locked her long legs around his thick neck, squirming under him as he worked his magic. Feeling her limbs quivering, he brought his head up and bit gently up her inner thigh, circling her clit

THESE SCANDALOUS STREETS

with his thumb as he did so. Coming to her heel, he sucked on the ball of her foot then licked up the arch of it. Turning his head, he pampered her other thigh and foot as well. When he turned his head toward her, the lower half of his face was glistening from the nectar of her sex. The light shining in from the hallway on his back caused him to look like a lion having just devoured a Gazelle's carcass, her juices mirroring the murdered animal's blood dripping from off his chin. Dakeemia massaged that small flap of meat that hid between her coochie lips. She bit down on her bottom lip and moaned, keeping her eyes interlocked with his as she pleased herself. Malakai stopped her from pleasuring herself, moving her delicate hand aside. He lifted her from up off the bed and carried her over to the wall where he held her up against it. Right then, he proceeded to suck on her swollen clit like it was an apple Jolly Rancher, his sexual prowess had her trying to climb the wall like Spider Woman.

"Uh uh." He grabbed a firm hold of her hips, causing the meat to seep between his strong masculine hands while he attended to his supper. "Mmmmhmmm." He was eating that pussy like it was shrimp fried rice.

"Ah, shit! Baby, I'm about to nut!" She threw her head back and shouted, showcasing the piercing in her tongue. "Yes! Yes! Yes! Fuck..." her face twisted into a hideous mask as she met The Big O, drenching her lover with her warm liquid. "Ughhh!" she shook like she was butt ass naked in a blizzard.

Malakai let his lady down from the wall and wiped his chin with the back of his fist. She led him to the bed where she shoved him onto his back and straddled him. Next, she traced his bullet wounds and stab wounds with her warm, wet tongue admiring the many tattoos of his body; most noticeably the one going across his abs. *Natural Born*

THESE SCANDALOUS STREETS

Hustlah, was there in big bold fancy letters. Dakeemia licked down the crevasse that separated her man's abs. When she reached his manhood it was already as hard as steel. Taking a hold of it, she swirled her tongue around the rim of its head. He gasped and moaned, anticipating his lover's enticing mouth. When he finally received it, he regretted spending the past eight years behind barbwire fences. Propping himself upon his elbows, he watched as his boo handled her business. Baby girl was whipping that head on him with a porn star's expertise, her mouth slobbering up and down his meat. The slurping and sucking sounds she made turned him on and caused his hardness to harden further. Seeing the faces he was making, she knew he was about to bless her with his seeds, so she pulled him from her lips. Right after, she wiped her mouth with the back of her hand, leaving his dick leaning to the side, glistening wet.

"Why you stop? I was 'bout to pop," he complained with a fixed frown.

"Uh uh, not yet, boo. I wanna feel you." Dakeemia turned her back on him and squatted. Lining her pussy up with his bulbous head, she slowly lowered herself onto it until it disappeared. She moved back and forth on his pole, making it disappear and reappear like a magic trick. Once she'd found her rhythm she sped up, throwing her fat ass into him, her buttocks smacking up against him.

Smack! Smack! Smack! Smack!

The chocolate goddess leaned forward and held his legs down into the bed. She closed her eyes, clenched her jaws and threw herself into him harder and faster. Malakai's nut sack swelled up and his babies soared up his dick. He lifted his head up from the pillow, twisting his face up, and holding her hips as she slammed down into him. Watching her ebony stretch marked ass collide into him caused his semen to build up and he felt himself about to explode.

"Ahhhh! I'ma 'bout to bust! Ssssss!"

"Nuh uh. Not yet. I'm almost there. Mmmmm." She licked and bit down at the corner of her bottom lip.

He closed his eyes and tried to think of something besides that bodacious ass of hers. He thought of clowns, old naked fat women, cartoons, and scenes from his favorite movies. Although he put up a good fight, in the end The Power of the V was just too much for him.

"Ahh! Yeah! Yes!" Dakeemia screamed excitedly.

"I can't hold it! Ahhhh! Fuckkkk!" Malakai made an ugly face as he grasped her hips and spilled his seeds inside of her womb, seeing some of it ooze out. "Uhhhhh!" The chocolate goddess came right behind him, drenching his lap with Passion's River. He fell flat out in bed with his big muscular arms lying spread out. His forehead rolled with sweat as he huffed and puffed, chest heaving up and down.

Dakeemia pulled the sheet over her as she laid her head against Malakai's chiseled chest. He wrapped his strong arms around her and kissed her on the forehead tenderly. They then closed their eyes.

"I love you." she told him saying some of the most powerful words on this earth.

"I love you, too," he uttered what every soul wanted to hear back, and with that, they met with sleep.

The next morning

Dakeemia's eyelids peeled open and she looked to the digital clock on the dresser. It was 10:47 A.M. She turned over in bed and the space where Malakai was lying was empty. She sucked her teeth and sat up, taking a roach end of

THESE SCANDALOUS STREETS

a blunt from the ashtray and lighting it up. She pulled smoke into her lungs and blew it out, tainting the air. A flicker of movement in her peripherals brought her attention to the bedroom doorway where she saw her man walking by in a Champion hoodie.

Where this nigga going? She thought to herself, sliding her pretty manicured feet into her slippers and wrapping herself in the Kimono. She headed into the kitchen and found Malakai looking through the cupboards. "What are you looking for?"

"Where you stash my guns at? They aren't where I put them before I got locked up," he said, still searching the cupboards with his cell phone to his ear.

"What chu need your guns for?" she asked.

"Yo', Zeal, I'll be down in a hot one." He disconnected the call and slipped his cell inside of his pocket, turning to Dakeemia. "What is this? Twenty questions? It's my shit and I want it," Malakai said copping a slight attitude.

She blew hot air from her nose and mouth, rolling her eyes with her arms folded across her chest. "Fine." She walked inside of the kitchen and took a butter knife from out of the drawer, approaching the old box television set in the living room. The TV didn't work but it served its purpose well. Using the knife, she pried open the joining halves of the television and separated them, four handguns came spilling out. Malakai stashed one of the guns at the small of his back and pulled his hood over his head.

"I'll be back," He pecked Dakeemia on the lips and headed out of the door. Once outside of the complex, he jogged across the street and hopped into the Escalade truck and Bizeal drove off.

THESE SCANDALOUS STREETS
***

"So this is the spot, huh?" Malakai asked from the backseat, taking pulls from a burning blunt. His lips were as black as his fingertips from smoking. Even behind the wall he was constantly getting faded.

"Yeah, this is it." Bizeal told him from the driver's seat. He too was peering up at the enormous apartment complex through the rearview mirror.

"Imagine the money that comes in and outta that mothafucka on a daily and nightly bases." Crazy stared at the complex through the back window.

"What they pushing out here?" Malakai inquired.

"From my understanding they got crack on one floor, heroin on another and weed on the last."

"You said some nigga named Romadal got this right." Malakai looked to Bizeal. "Well, how in the hell he got this shit on smash and them Boys ain't crashed the party?"

"Sheeiiiiit, that muscle head nigga got Five Owe in pocket."

"Is that right?" He passed the L up front to Crazy.

"Real Life."

Malakai hopped out of the car and folded his arms across his chest, looking up at the huge apartment building. It looked more like an old hospital than a complex. *If I take this mothafucka over, I can be seeing hella grips. I could get this thang popping. Execute the Top Dawg, take his workers under my deodorant, and move stupid work*, he thought to himself as he grinned and nodded, massaging his chin. *Yeah, I'ma 'bout to pull the panties off this bitch and fuck her, fa sho'*, he grinned mischievously as he rubbed his hands together.

THESE SCANDALOUS STREETS

"Pardon me, but just how in the fuck do you suggest that we take over this big ass complex?" Bizeal tilted his head back and allow smoke to billow from his nose and mouth. His eyes were red webbed and glassy, he was as high as giraffe pussy. "This mothafucka got like I don't know how many hittas. And this nigga Romadal is papered up out of the game."

"He ain't lying; my nigga'z money is as long as my dick." Crazy threw in his two cents. His eyes were hooded and pink from getting blowed.

Bizeal shot him a look like *Nigga if you don't stop over exaggerating.*

"We need somebody that can give us the 411 on things, who's who in their organization. With that information we could take out the muscle, hit their asses hard and fast." He took the blunt, holding it pinched between his thumb and pointer finger. "We get rid of his killas and that'll leave his pussy open to a fuck, ya feel me?"

"We'd need somebody that we can flip for some info." Bizeal chimed back in.

"Yeah, but who?" Malakai massaged his chin, while he held the smoldering L wedged in between his fingers in the other hand.

"Yo' any of y'all gotta seven?" a scraggily crack head by the name of Tyrone clawed at his neck. He was as black as the night and had white shit at the corners of his mouth. The wife beater he sported was raggedy and as dirty as the one Bruce Willis wore in Die Hard.

Bizeal and Malakai exchanged glances and smiles.

Malakai had the crack head snap photos of all of Romadal's lieutenants and hittas. In order for the hustler to seize the Sheridan he was going to have to take out these very individuals. This would make it easier for him to slip in and dethrone the kingpin. After all how safe was a king without his pawns to protect him. Malakai made a list of the niggaz he had to execute on his crawl up the ladder to Top Dawg. He found satisfaction in knowing that once the last name was crossed out he'd be *That Nigga* again.

Sunday afternoon

Malakai came out of church with his grandmother's arm looped within his own. He opened the front passenger door for her Mercedes and stashed her inside before hopping in on the driver side.
"I was thinking me and you should head over to Denny's and get us a couple of those Grand Slams." Malakai told her. "How about it? My treat," He tried to entice her to go.
"IHOP, and it's my treat." Mrs. Williams smiled.
"Mrs. Williams, you drive a hard bargain." Malakai replied pulling into traffic. "IHOP it is, beautiful."
"So what do you plan on doing with yourself now that you're home?" she asked her youngest grandson.
"I got some things lined up, networked with a couple of people when I got out."
"Humph, I know what that means."
Malakai blew hard and rolled his eyes. He wasn't up to hearing any lectures that afternoon. "And what is that, momma?"
"Those streets," she told him. "You gon' run your ass right back out there to them. I really don't understand you young men today, you're so loyal to those streets but she's not to you. She doesn't show any love to any of you, but still, there you go running back to her as soon as those white folks turn ya loose."
"Momma, ain't nobody looking to hiring an ex-con."

THESE SCANDALOUS STREETS

"You don't have to work for anyone, son. You can be your own boss, start your own business. We're rich or have you forgotten? Your brother left us with plenty of money."

"Momma, that's your money. Blessyn left that to you." He took his hand off of the steering wheel and pointed to her. "I got some change of my own and with that I plan on making my own way in this world."

"I'ma pray for you, son."

"Don't waste your time, momma. God don't got no love for niggaz like me."

Mrs. Williams stared at her grandson for a while. It was then that she realized that he was too far gone for even The Creator to salvage.

"The streets don't love you baby, they take you away from the people that do."

Malakai focused his attention back on the road, commanding the luxury vehicle with one hand, frown fixed on his face. He knew what his grandmother was saying was true but truthfully he didn't give a shit. The game owed him and he was going to get her for all that she was worth.

THESE SCANDALOUS STREETS
Chapter Seven

Tyson stood out on the curb with his luggage at his feet, occasionally glancing at the clock on his cell phone. It was two thirty in the afternoon, twenty minutes passed the time that the chauffer from Big Willie records was supposed to pick him up and he was getting antsy. Having growing frustrated with the wait, he scrolled through his recent calls to find the number of the driver. Just as he was about to hit him up a Lincoln Town Car limousine pulled up before him, stealing his attention. The driver side door swung open and Keith hopped out, rounding the rear of the trunk. He popped it open and lifted it up, casting his hostile eyes on him.

"You Tyson?" Keith asked with a snobby attitude.

"Yeah." Tyson answered like *What the fuck is this nigga'z problem?* He stood there for a time like he was waiting for something to happen.

"Fuck you waiting for, nigga? Toss your shit in so we can go." he grumbled, throwing his hand toward the empty trunk.

Tyson looked at him like he'd lost his goddamn mind, taking a deep breath. He could already see that he wasn't going to like this mothafucka, not even a little bit. After depositing his luggage into the trunk and closing it, he made his way around to the back passenger door. He stood there looking from the door to Keith who was giving him the evil eye.

"Humph." Keith turned his nose up at him. "If you think I'm about to open that door for you then you got another thang coming, homeboy." He opened the driver side door and slid inside of the whip, slamming the door shut.

"Old bitch ass nigga," Tyson said before ducking off inside of the limo. They were pulling off when he was

THESE SCANDALOUS STREETS

picking up the small remote to the Bose stereo and turning it on. He flipped through the channels until he reached Rick Ross's *Rich Forever* featuring John Legend. He smeared caviar over crackers and ate them. Next, he poured himself a flute of Ace of Spades and sipped it, savoring the fine taste as he watched the scenery change from behind the black tinted window. The landscape changed from the houses of the ghetto, liquor stores, and mom and pop businesses to the tall buildings and well lit streets of downtown Los Angeles.

The stretched Lincoln pulled into the parking garage of a tall black building. Keith parked into a stall specially reserved for the CEO of Big Willie Records. Tyson brushed the crumbs from his shirt and killed the stereo. He downed the last of the bubbly and hopped out of the limousine, following Keith to the elevator.

Ding!

The elevator chimed when it arrived on the 12th floor. Its doors parted allowing its occupants to exit. They made their way passed the security guard at the front desk that had his feet propped upon the counter running some weak game down to some chick on the other end of the phone. Once he saw Keith giving him the evil eye he sat up and acted like he was giving someone directions to the building.

Tyson marveled the platinum and gold plaques that aligned the walls of the hallway they traveled. The further he and Keith journeyed down the corridor the louder the voice grew of someone talking over the phone.

"I sent my man to pick him up. They should be here in a minute." Showtime said into the phone. He looked up to find Tyson and Keith entering his office. "Yo', here your boy go." He out stretched the telephone to his newest employee and he took it.

THESE SCANDALOUS STREETS

"Who is this?" Tyson asked, holding the phone to his chest.

"Grief." Showtime answered.

"What's up, Grief?"

"Nothing, just seeing if you touched down yet."

"Yeah, I'm good."

"Remember our agreement, youngster."

"How could I forget? My loved one's lively hood is riding on it."

"Let me speak back to Showtime."

"Yo?" Showtime said into the phone. "Yeah, I gotchu, OG, don't even worry about it. We're going to take good care of him. Alright, peace." He hung up the telephone. "Tyson, right?" he out stretched his hand.

"Yeah," Tyson shook his hand.

"Showtime," He smiled, flashing his gold capped fangs.

"Yeah, I know."

"That tall Kareem Abdul Jabbar looking brotha in the corner there is my uncle and bodyguard, Keith."

"That brotha there has got a serious attitude problem."

"Have a seat," Showtime held his hand out towards the chair beyond his desk. Tyson sat down. "You'll have to excuse my people. He's not too enthusiastic about Big Willie hiring new employees."

"Well, if someone was on their job I wouldn't be here, now would I?"

Keith scowled and clenched his jaws. He clenched his fists and started in on Tyson, but a motion of Showtime's hand stayed him.

"No, you're right. My people fucked up." Showtime admitted. "If it wasn't for our slip up you wouldn't be sitting before me." He lay back in his chair putting the tips of his fingers and thumbs together. "Can I offer you a drink, soda,

THESE SCANDALOUS STREETS

water, champagne? I got liquor on the mini bar there." He pointed to the mini-bar which was sitting to the side against the wall.

"Nah, I'm good." Tyson said staring at the large portrait mounted to the wall above Showtime's desk. It was a very lifelike painting of Blessyn. He was sitting on a throne wearing a diamond studded gold crown. A lion's head rested on his shoulder. He held a spear that had feathers tied around its neck. A beautiful chocolate goddess lay at his feet with her arms wrapped around his leg. "That's a nice painting."

Showtime looked over his shoulder at the portrait. "Yeah, that's my man Blessyn. Lotta cats argue that Big, or Pac was the best but to us he wears the crown."

"Rest in peace," Tyson crossed his heart in the name of the Lord.

"Alright, let's get down to business," Showtime said, removing some paperwork from his drawer and laying it before him along with a pen.

"What's this?" he asked, looking over the paperwork.

"A few things you need to sign," Showtime informed him. "It's just paperwork stating that you're an employee of Big Willie Records. There's also information on the medical and dental insurance plan we have."

"What if something were to happen to me while I'm out there on the job?"

"If anything were to happen to you, knock on wood," he knocked on the desk top. "Big Willie would take care of all of your burial expenses."

"Cool."

"Just sign here, here, and there," Showtime pointed to the areas on the paperwork for Tyson to sign. Once he had given his John Hancock on the documents, Showtime went behind

THESE SCANDALOUS STREETS

him signing his. Once he was done he stacked the papers neatly on the side of his desk.

"How much are y'all paying me?"

"That's right, I almost forgot. Your salary is $3,000 dollars a week."

Tyson whistled at the amount of money he'd be making under Big Willie Records. He had made more out in the streets jacking mothafuckas, but he had no idea he could make that kind of money squaring up. At first he was expecting a security guard's salary but three grand a week was pretty sweet.

Keith laughed and said, "That's lunch money. I give my bitch that lil' change to cop her a bag with."

Tyson looked over his shoulder at him and cut his eyes. He could tell that the old school gangster was going to be a thorn in his side. "What's up, my nigga? You need that, or something?"

"What chu gone do, lil' nigga?" Keith took a bite of an orange.

"I'ma hop out this chair and kick your fucking ass, bitch!"

Keith pulled his gun from its holster and sat it down on the file cabinet, and tossed what was left of his orange into the trashcan.

"Let's go." He smiled wickedly, gesturing Tyson to come on with both hands.

He hopped out of his chair and was about to approach him when Showtime grabbed him by the shoulder. "Y'all knock that shit off, man! This is a place of business." Showtime barked.

Y'all wanna compare dick sizes then do that shit outside. As a matter of fact, unc', do me a favor and take a walk."

Keith holstered his gun and moved for the door.

THESE SCANDALOUS STREETS

"That's right, do as your daddy tells you." Tyson taunted him.

He stopped and looked over his shoulder, shooting the thug a dirty look.

"Unc', gon' and relax in the lobby." Showtime told him. "I'll call you once I'm done here."

He walked behind his desk and picked up a bulletproof vest. Next, he held it on top of the desk and knocked on it. "This bulletproof Kevlar vest is strong enough to stop a 12 gauge shotgun round." He laid the bulletproof vest down and pulled open his desk drawer. Inside there were two black .45 automatics, a box of shells, and two magazines. He handed Tyson the guns and placed the rest of the items on the desk.

Tyson inspected both of the weapons, checking their magazines and their sights.

".45 ACP, they hold fifteen shells a piece." Showtime informed him on the guns.

"Are they clean?" Tyson asked, flipping the twin weapons back and forth with his fingers inside of the trigger guards. The guns looked like blurs in his palms he was spinning them bitches around so fast, up, down and all around they went. He was doing fancy maneuvers with them like a skilled gunfighter would. Abruptly, he caught them in his hands and aimed them around the office with a serious expression plastered across his face. He imagined himself firing the deadly weapons on a couple of niggaz looking to snatch up his Treasure.

"Clean. No bodies." He assured him. "Now, on your paper work it says unarmed bodyguard, that's 'cause you have a felony and the shit would be illegal for me to give you one. But if you just so happen to get knocked with them bitches, you didn't get them from me."

"I gotchu."

THESE SCANDALOUS STREETS

"Grief tells me you know Karate."

"I know a lil' something, something."

"Not one to toot your own horn, huh?"

"Can I meet my client now?" he asked, like he wasn't trying to get into all of that.

"Sure, follow me." Showtime got the point and rose from his chair.

When Tyson crossed the threshold into the studio the first person he saw was Dead Beat, Big Willie Records in house producer and engineer, sitting behind the boards. All the switches, gadgets, and neon lights on the boards made it look like something inside of a spaceship.

Dead Beat had his eyes closed and was nodding his head to a soulful track as an angelic voice song over it from behind the glass of the recording booth. He was a slim white dude with a thick goatee. His entire body was covered with tattoos; most noticeable was the one going across his fingers, *Dead Beat*. His hair was greasy and slicked back. He wore a derby, a blue plaid shirt on top of a thermal, and stone washed jeans with a wallet chain attached.

Zack Callahan aka Dead Beat lived a fast and hard life. While attending college for musical engineering, he partied and experimented with weed and prescription drugs that eventually led to him shooting heroin. Dead Beat's studies slacked and before long he was dropped by the school. He ran the streets drugging and slumming for years, until that one faithful night he was visited by a man he swore was Jesus Christ. Dead Beat broke down. He dropped to his knees at the man's feet crying and praying until he disappeared. The next day he checked himself into a rehabilitation center. It was there that he met Showtime's nephew. The two of them clicked instantly having shared the same interests in music. Dead Beat played him some of his instrumentals and he fell in love with them. He hadn't heard anything like it. The white boy had a sound of his own. The kid got on the jack with his uncle and the rest was history.

"What's up, kid?" Showtime slapped hands with the producer and embraced him.

"What it is, big Showtime?" he replied with a smile. "Ain't shit, just laying down a track with ya girl." He said, referring to Treasure Gold who was the one projecting that angelic voice from the recording booth. Her hands held the headphones to her ears as she crooned into the microphone, oblivious to the presence of the guests.

"Who is this?" Dead Beat asked, referring to Tyson.

"Tyson." He introduced himself, out stretching his hand.

"Dead Beat." He shook his hand.

"Dead Beat, huh? Why they call you that?" Tyson inquired.

"You don't take care of your kids, or something?"

Dead Beat and Showtime laughed.

"Nah, they call my man Dead Beat 'cause he be killing the tracks," Showtime informed him. "You know, bodying the beats."

"Dead Beat, huh? Nice." Tyson nodded in approval of the name.

Showtime held down a switch and spoke into the intercom that was linked to the recording booth. "Yo', Treasure, get out here, girl. I got somebody out here I want you to meet!"

When Treasure stepped out of the recording booth into full view Tyson gasped. Through his eyes it appeared as if she was moving in slow motion, one hooker boot at a time. She was visually stunning, and more gorgeous than she was on television and in magazines. She had a caramel complexion and a body most women had to visit a plastic surgeon for. The songstress oozed with sex appeal that could draw any man in like quick sand. At the moment she was wearing D&G shades, a black leather motorcycle jacket, a red plaid shirt which she wore tucked in and blue jeans that looked like they were painted on. Her long jet black hair was pulled back in a ponytail. She had a butterfly tattoo on the side of her brow and a diamond studded nose piercing. Big gold Bamboo earrings hung from her earlobes and a gold necklace with her name in fancy lettering flooded with diamonds decorated her neck.

"Tyson, Treasure. Treasure, Tyson…your bodyguard." Showtime made the introductions, sweeping his hand back and forth between them.

"Hi, how are you doing?" Tyson said in his sexiest voice. He took Treasure's hand when she extended it and kissed it gently, making sure to keep eye contact while doing so.

"Look at this suave, mothafucka." The head honcho at Big Willie records chuckled and nudged Dead Beat.

"Alright," Treasure replied to Tyson, rolling her eyes and snatching away her hand.

He eyed her seductively and licked his lips like LL Cool J.

Treasure took a bottle of Fiji water from the small refrigerator and plopped down on the black leather sofa.

"Well, me and Dead Beat will leave you two alone to get acquainted." Showtime motioned for the producer to follow him.

"Yeah, I need a cigarette break anyway." Dead Beat pulled a cigarette from the wrinkled pack of Camel's stashed inside his shirt pocket.

As Showtime and Dead Beat left the studio, Tyson pulled up a chair and sat on it backwards, facing who he felt was the woman of his dreams.

THESE SCANDALOUS STREETS

"So, uh, is Treasure the same name on your birth certificate?" he questioned.

Treasure took a drink of water. "Boy is your mack weak, Goldie. Look, Tyson, let's get this understood, you're cute and all but I don't fuck around with the help, feel me? If you're gonna work for me then we're gonna keep things on a business tip."

"Man, you think I'm cute? I've been called handsome before but never cute. Cute is normally reserved for puppies and new born babies."

"Nigga, that's all you got from what I just said?" she looked upon him disbelievingly.

"That and you calling me Goldie," He smiled, dimpling his cheeks. "Believe me you won't even realize you've been gamed when I sink my talons in you."

"I heard that hot shit."

"Nah, on the real, I heard you and you're right. Us getting involved would only complicate things. Through my experiences mixing business with pleasure has always led to a disaster, so I can respect that."

"As long as we understand each other."

"Now, since we're gonna be seeing each other for the next two years, I figure we should get to know one another a lil' better. Agree?"

"Fair enough."

"What's your favorite color? Your birthday? Who was your first kiss?"

"Violet, January 11th, and Maurice Kyle."

"Alright, ask me something?"

"Like what?"

"Anything."

"Okay. How long have you been in the business?"

"This is my first job."

THESE SCANDALOUS STREETS

"You're kidding, right?"

"No. This is my first gig."

"Well, what kind of training do you have?"

"None, really," He shamelessly admitted. "I've studied mixed martial arts since I was like eight. I thought chu already knew this. They didn't tell you?" he frowned.

"No. I was hoping to get someone with experience." Treasure spoke honestly. "I mean, what did my daddy do, pull your name outta hat?"

"I suppose you don't know I'm a convicted felon and that I met your father in prison either?"

"No, please enlighten me." She frowned, screwing the cap on her Fiji water and sitting up.

Tyson relayed all the details of what happened back in prison and the agreement he'd made with her father.

"Wow."

"Yep, so I gotta make sure you're nice and healthy." He stared at Treasure as if he could see through her D&G shades, cracking a sexy smile.

"What?" she tried to conceal a jovial expression.

"So, when are you gonna stop fronting and take off those shades? You're not fooling anybody trying to hide that shiner."

"How do you know what's behind these shades? You got X-ray vision, or something?"

"Yep, come on now. Take them off and let me see."

Treasure snatched off her shades, exposing her black eye. "Happy now?"

"Nope," He frowned. Seeing her face bruised like that pissed him the fuck off. He hated when cats put their hands on women, it really got under his skin. He didn't know exactly what happened to her the night she received that black eye, but he wished he was there to put hands on the cock sucka that gave it to her. "What happened?"

She slid the shades back on and said, "We here at Big Willie Records have what we like to call a 'don't ask don't tell policy'."

He nodded his head.

"I Griff you. Wow, the beautiful Treasure Gold. Wait 'til I tell Cody about this."

"Who's Cody?"

"My lil' cousin, he whacks off to your poster every day."

"Aww, how cute, how old is he? Fifteen? Sixteen?"

"Twenty-three."

"Ewww."

Tyson laughed his ass off.

***

"I'm not feeling this shit, man." Keith paced the floor of Showtime's office. "You put this young nigga on the team now it's gonna look like I'm not doing my job, like I'm not handling my business over here!"

"Lower your voice in my office and calm your hostile black ass down," Showtime spoke from behind his desk, where he sat with his hands clasped in his lap. "Far as I can see the kid is okay. And from the way the old man says he handled those fools back in the joint, I know he'll have no problem protecting baby girl. Look at it like this, in a year he'll be outta your hair and things will be back how they were."

Keith poured himself a drink at the mini-bar. He sat in the chair before his nephew's desk and took a sip from his glass.

THESE SCANDALOUS STREETS

"What's up with chu and this nigga Grief?" he asked. "You didn't have to bring this punk on just 'cause he said so. You're running this, you could have told old boy to go fuck himself."

"The old man is just someone that I admire." Showtime told the truth. "An old school player that lives by a set of old school rules, and follows a code that dates back to since before I was born. In this day and age that's rare. You're from his era, I'm sure you can respect that."

"You're right," Keith agreed with a nod. "They don't breed them like us anymore. The real niggaz of the world have damn near become like the dinosaurs." He took a sip of his drink.

"How is that?" Showtime asked curiously.

"We, too, are almost extinct."

THESE SCANDALOUS STREETS

Chapter Eight

The stretch Lincoln rolled through the gates of Showtime's estate and parked in the white cobblestone, horseshoe driveway. Keith opened the backdoor of the limousine and everyone hopped out. Tyson looked up at the enormous mansion in awe like a kid at Disney World. The place was surrounded by rich green acres of grass and lit up with bright lights. From the outside looking in you would think some kind of ball was taking place inside.

A short, dark skinned butler with graying hair and a goatee pushed a luggage-cart outside and loaded Tyson's things onto it.

"Beautiful, isn't she?" Showtime smiled and nudged Tyson, focused on his home.

"Gorgeous." Tyson replied, observing the mansion.

"Yo', man. I'll check you in the morning," Keith told Showtime before he was pulled along up the steps by an Asian Amazon.

"That old nigga done bit off more than he can chew." Showtime said, watching the healthy behind on the Amazon sway from side to side as she made her way up the steps.

"Follow me, sir. I'll show you to your room." The butler told Tyson.

***

"And this is your room, Mr. McGowan." The butler told Tyson after he'd unloaded his luggage.

Tyson walked across the floor of the huge bedroom to the glass double-doors that led out to the terrace. He twisted the golden handles and pulled open the doors. The fresh, cool air of the outside rushed in, washing over his face and

THESE SCANDALOUS STREETS

body. He took a deep breath and exhaled. Stepping out onto the terrace, he looked around at the scattered homes in the distance. They were just as appealing as the mansion he was staying in. Their backyard's had a pool, tennis court, and basketball court, also.

"Wow." Tyson said under his breath. He turned around to the butler. "What's your name, OG?"

"Preston," the butler responded. "Preston Courtingbeck, sir."

"You mind showing me the rest of this place, Preston?"

"As you wish, Mr. McGowan," he replied. "Follow me."

Preston showed Tyson every bedroom inside the mansion. He commented on the themes of the rooms and where the furniture, tile, rugs, curtains, and covers were imported from. The mansion had fifteen bedrooms, two studies and six bathrooms. And Tyson saw every last one.

"I know I lost fifteen, twenty pounds walking around here." Tyson said, taking off his jacket. "Y'all got everything in here except a gym." Preston smiled. "Get the fuck outta here." He looked at him disbelievingly.

"Right this way, Mr. McGowan." Preston motioned for him to follow.

***

Preston flipped on a light-switch and gave life to a gymnasium half the size of a football field. It was equipped with every pound of weight and exercise machine you could think of. At the end of each wall were 50" flat-screens that came on as soon as the light-switch was flipped. Martin Scorsese's *Raging Bull* played on the LED widescreens.

Tyson threw his jacket over a weight bench. He removed his shirt and sneakers and approached the blue Ever Last

THESE SCANDALOUS STREETS

punching bag that hung from the ceiling. Next, he pushed the punching bag hard and it swung back on him. He moved from side to side avoiding the bag as it swung forward and backwards for his head.

"I'll leave you two alone." Preston smirked before leaving the gymnasium.

Tyson assaulted the bag, throwing punches, knees, and kicks into it. The bag rocked back and forth as if it was struggling to break loose from the chain that bound it to the ceiling. He attacked the bag with the intensity of a fighter training to fight his greatest opponent, sweat rolled down his face and body as he tore into the bag. He threw one last kick into it with all of his might before sitting on the mat and pulling his feet into him. Tyson breathed heavily as he wiped the sweat from his forehead with the back of his hand.

He heard someone applauding from the doorway and turned around. It was Showtime. He tossed him a white towel and Tyson got to his feet, wiping down his face and chest.

"I'd hate to see what you would do to flesh and bone." He clapped with a smile; gold fangs twinkling. "What exactly is that style called?"

"A lil' some of everything; mixed martial arts."

"Word? I might just have to keep you on. Come join me for a drink."

***

Tyson and Showtime stood out on the terrace looking out at the stars while taking sips of Cognac.

"So, what's your story, Tyson?" Showtime asked, staring up into the sky.

THESE SCANDALOUS STREETS

"There's not much of a story to tell. I'm just a kid from South Central. I jacked and stole tryna come up. I ended up doing four years in the joint and here I am; chopping it up with a multimillionaire."

"Street nigga, huh?"

"From what I've read you are too."

The CEO of Big Willie records took a sip of his drink and hissed when the strong liquor engulfed his throat. "Yeah, I started out with a pack and a dream. I grind rain, sleet, or snow and parlayed those yellow tops into what you see before you." He swept his hand over the vast land that was the fruits of his labor. "But let's keep that between me and you. The last thing a nigga need is an indictment."

"Aye." Tyson pretended to zip his lips shut. "Your secret is safe with me."

"My man." He cracked a gold fanged smile, dapping him up.

"Treasure says you're from Harlem."

"Yezzir, born and raised, the Douglass projects. That's where I grew up and threw up." He grinned proudly. "Like you, I was throwing stones at the penitentiary, and eventually they let my black ass in."

"You did a lil' time?" a line formed across his forehead.

"Two years." He held up two fingers. "Fighting a murder beef, the man was looking to gas my skinny poor behind. Twenty years old and I was scared as shit. I can't even front. OG cat that was my cellie gave me The Holy Bible and I buried my face in it. I attended church every chance I got, praying and scuffing my knees up for the Lord."

"Niggaz turn religious when they're facing hell or jail. Believe me I know." Tyson took a sip of Cognac.

"You ain't never lied, fam." Showtime chuckled. "Anyway, every day before lights out I got down on my knees and

THESE SCANDALOUS STREETS

I said, 'Lord, this is Jarvis again. I know you're tired of seeing me on my knees every night but I need your help again. If you pull me outta this one, I promise to keep my nose clean.' I'll tell you, our God is a merciful one 'cause he yanked my ass outta that fire."

"Here's to our freedom." Tyson clinked glasses with his new boss. They took a sip. "How did you stumble upon Treasure?"

"I was out in Oakland on tour with Blessyn. We stopped at a gas station slash mini mart to get a lil' bottle of something and baby girl was there slinging her CD out the trunk of her car. She gave me one of her CDs, but I didn't listen to it. I tossed it to the side in a pile with the rest of the demos I got while on the road. I figured it was trash. Hell, I get thousands of demos every day at my office and they aren't worth a hot cup of piss. About a month later I'm rolling in the car with Blessyn and this song *Never Again* comes on. The most beautiful voice I've ever heard came spilling outta those speakers. I ask Blessyn who it was and he says its old girl from the gas station. See, Blessyn had grown tired of the bullshit they were spinning on the radio, so he picked through my demo pile for something fresh to listen to." He cleared his throat with a fist to it. "I damn near broke my neck scrambling to the phone to call my pilot to fly me out to The Bay. I made it down there with the contracts and a quarter million dollar check and signed baby girl on the spot." He took a sip of Cognac.

"So, what's the real untold story with homegirl, man?" Tyson asked with a serious look in his eyes. "She got the mafia or some crazy ex-boyfriend after her?"

Although he already had an idea of what happened with Treasure he wanted to know if he was biting off more than he could chew.

THESE SCANDALOUS STREETS

"Nah, nothing like that," the Top Dawg of Big Willie records assured him. "We just need the extra help around here. Besides, Treasure has never had her own bodyguard and it's about time she got one. With your skills I'm sure she'll be safe with you."

"Are you sure? I'm tryna see exactly what I'm dealing with here."

"Trust me. Besides a bunch of wild ass teenage girls and a few groupie ass niggaz, you don't have anything to worry about."

Tyson swallowed the last of his Cognac. "Alright, I'ma call it a night."

"Alright, Duke." He slapped hands with his newest employee. Once Tyson was gone, he sat his empty glass on ledge and lit up a Cuban cigar, puffing out smoke. He blew a cloud into the air and continued to marvel his estate.

The empire that crack built.

***

Treasure lay in a nice hot bath sipping a glass of wine while reading a romance novel. Like all women she wanted to meet her knight in shining armor. She yearned to be swept off of her feet by some suave, charming mothafucka. She wanted the same as Savannah Montgomery, the middle aged white woman in the pages of her cheesy book. She wanted her ideal man to come riding into her life on his white horse. With his ripped muscles and strong chiseled jaw, he'd come galloping up with his long hair swinging in the summer breeze. His body would be glistening under the warm rays of the sun. He would dismount his horse, rip open her blouse and force her onto the sand, where he would make passionate love to her.

THESE SCANDALOUS STREETS

Goosebumps ran up Treasure's arms just thinking about her dream guy. He wouldn't resemble the Fabio looking hunk on the cover of her book though. However, he would possess his muscles and he would have long hair. Only it would be in cornrows or dreads. And he would be tatted up like Travis Barker. He would be tough and aggressive; a take charge kind of guy. People would fear and respect him. She loved bad boys so he would definitely have to be a thug, with a sensitive side he only showed to her. He would be a beast in the streets as well as in the sheets.

Treasure played Frankenstein in her head, assembling the body parts she'd need to create her perfect male specimen. She would put Morris Chestnut's head on top of Dwayne 'The Rock' Johnson's body. She would give him Lil' Wayne's dreadlocks and Tupac Shakur's thug mentality. He would be hung like Tommy Lee and have the sex prowess of a porno stud: Jake Steed, Mr. Marcus, or Wesley Pipes; either of those would do.

Treasure's mind drifted off to Tyson. He was tall, dark, and handsome. Plus, he had an incredible body and crazy sex appeal. She could tell that he was thuggish and had some hood in him, which only made her even more attracted to him, because her man couldn't be a square. If it weren't for him being her bodyguard she probably would have given him a chance, just to see where things would go. God only knew how much she craved for the touch of a man. She hadn't been with anyone since Trip. He had been her first and so far her last.

Knocks at the door snapped Treasure out of her daydreaming.

"Yeah?" She called out.

"Hey, it's Tyson. I just wanted to say goodnight, Ms. Gold."

THESE SCANDALOUS STREETS

"Goodnight, Mr. McGowan." Treasure smiled.

***

"Yeah, baby, I'm exhausted. I'm just gonna crash in Jarvis' guest bedroom." Keith said into his cell as he removed his coat and loosened his tie. "I miss you and the kids, too. Well, look," he glanced at his Rolex. "It's a lil' after eleven, I can just call a taxi to take me home and leave my car here. Yes, it is kind of late but if you guys want me home I'll go ahead and send for a car. Are you sure? All right, I love you, too. Give the girls a kiss for me. Goodnight." He hung up. He unbuckled his belt and let his slacks drop to the floor.

Keith presented himself as a hardened criminal while out in the streets. Cats only felt his aggressiveness and the chill from his freezer box of a heart. Only when he was around his wife and kids did he show his kinder, gentler side. When they were around he was soft and as sweet as cotton-candy. It was safe to say that his family was his kryptonite.

Keith stood beside the bed with a rock hard dick. The China doll stepped to him, wrapping her arms around his neck. She was wearing a see-through black robe that left very little to the imagination. She kissed him intensely then shoved him back on the bed. *It was about to go down!*

Chapter Nine
Next morning

Tyson, Treasure and Showtime sat at the kitchen table eating breakfast prepared by Preston. There were blue berry pancakes, eggs, bacon, hash browns and pitchers of apple and orange juice.

"So what's the day's agenda?" Tyson asked, taking a bite of crisp bacon.

"We gotta pick my homegirl up from the airport. Tonight will be just a girls night out, you know?" Treasure took a sip from her glass of apple juice.

"What about the recording session with Stevie Ray?" Showtime inquired, looking up from the Los Angeles Times newspaper.

"Oh, that's next week, we're supposed to do it at his place."

"I didn't know you mess with Stevie Ray." Tyson interjected.

"Yeah, we're supposed to record this duet together."

"I like that movie he was in. What was it called?" Tyson snapped his fingers trying to recall.

"Triumphant." Showtime told him, folding his news paper.

"Yeah, that's it: Triumphant. That was a hell of a movie." Tyson nodded, remembering when he first saw the film.

"Isn't that the one where he's left paralyzed from the waist down from a football injury and he has to go through rehabilitation?" Treasure took a bite of eggs.

"That's the one." Showtime replied, picking up his glass of orange juice. "Homie can act."

"That movie was powerful; very inspirational." Treasure nodded. "It reminded me a lot of Rocky, except paralysis

THESE SCANDALOUS STREETS

was his adversary and not Apollo. So, what chu got going today, Big Show dog?" *Roof! Roof! Roof! Roof!* She barked like a dog.

Showtime chuckled and said, "Nothing, I've gotta couple things I have to take care at the office but that's it."

"Oh, alright."

"I'ma go ahead and get ready." Tyson tapped Treasure.

Keith walked through the door just as Tyson was heading out, bumping his shoulder. He turned around scowling with his nostrils flaring. He was about to put hands on him until Treasure spoke up. "Don't pay him any mind, Tyson. He's just tryna get under your skin." She tightened her jaws and gave Keith an expression that he read as *knock it the fuck off.*

Tyson took a deep breath causing his chest to heave up and down. Closing his eyes and blowing hot air from his nostrils, he calmed himself down.

"I'ma go and get dressed." He told the crooner before heading out of the door.

"Looks like you've got yourself a lil' lovers' quarrel, T." Showtime told Treasure with chuckled.

"Fuck that nigga!" Keith spat with envious eyes before pulling out a chair and sitting down.

"Here you go, sir." Preston sat a plate of breakfast before him and poured him a glass of orange juice.

"Keith, you really need to knock it off with that Alpha Male crap." Treasure scolded him like a single mother would her teenage son.

"Whatever." He failed a hand and stuffed a napkin within the collar of his shirt, preparing to eat.

"*Whatever* my ass, excuse me," Treasure shot up from the table.

THESE SCANDALOUS STREETS

"Treas, I..." Keith grabbed her arm but she snatched away, making her way out of the kitchen, as hot as fish grease.

"You done pissed The First Lady off." Showtime smirked, looking at him like *See what you done did?*

"I know lil' momma ain't sweating old boy like that." Keith looked at him like *Say it ain't so.*

"Who knows?" Showtime shrugged and poured maple syrup on his pancakes.

***

Treasure got dressed in a sleeveless gray shimmery sweater with a ruffled collar, black skintight spandex jeans, and black knee high leather pointy toe leather boots. She put on her platinum and black diamond earrings, a black diamond bracelet and a 14k black diamond and platinum ring. She picked up her Clutch bag and crossed the hall to her bodyguard's bedroom, lifting her fist to the door.

Knock! Knock! Knock!

A moment later Treasure heard the locks come undone and then the door being pulled open. A thick fog rolled out and the humid air rushed out into the hall. Tyson stepped forward wearing a bath towel, his chocolate form beaded in water. A very turned on Treasure took the thug in from head to toe. His body was muscular and well defined. His chest was ripped and his abs were rock solid. His body looked like someone had gotten a huge stone and chiseled his physique out of it. The tattoos that covered his body only added to his sex appeal. He had a rosary beaded necklace over his chest; the famous clown masks on his left peck with the saying *Laugh now, Cry later* below it, a red bandana that measured from his shoulder to his right peck, and *Low Bottoms* in Old English letters across his stomach.

THESE SCANDALOUS STREETS

Treasure licked her lips as she eyed Tyson like a thirsty kitten. *Damn, check baby out,* she thought. *Lord have mercy, the things I would do to you.* She bit her bottom lip, fanning herself with an imaginary fan, looking all hot and bothered.

Tyson cracked a one sided smile seeing this, "What's up, Treasure?"

"Huh?" She asked, snapping out of it. "Oh…yeah, I gotta pee."

"She's all yours, I'ma gon' and get dressed." He brushed passed her, but turned around once she called him.

"Tyson, do you drink milk?"

He laughed. "Plenty, why?"

"No reason, just curious."

I guess milk really does do a body good, Treasure thought as she walked into the bathroom. Tyson watched her fat ass jiggle on her way inside making a face of a nigga that had been stabbed. Once the door closed he went on about his business.

It must be jelly 'cause jam don't shake like that, he retreated to his bedroom and closed the door shut behind him.

***

Tyson put on his Kobe Bryant Lakers Jersey, which he wore over his Kevlar bulletproof vest, a pair of starched Levis 501 jeans and purple and yellow All-star Chuck Taylor Converses. He threw on a matching Lakers new era snapback and secured his twin .45s into their holsters before putting on his black bubble coat. He made his way down the steps and into the living room where Treasure awaited him.

"You look nice." She complimented him with a smile, taking in his digs.

THESE SCANDALOUS STREETS

"Thanks. You look beautiful as well." He projected a sexy smile.

"Aww, thank you, Tyson," She said.

"So, where are we headed?" he held open the door for her.

"LAX." She replied crossing the threshold.

"Los Angeles airport here we come." He closed the door shut behind them as they left.

***

Tyson looked from the windshield to the rearview mirror where he saw Treasure focused on the screen of her cell phone typing.

"So what's up with homeboy? He gotta death wish or something? 'Cause these twin .45s will grant it."

"Who?" her forehead crinkled wondering who he was talking about.

"Old head." He shot her a look like she should know exactly who the fuck he was talking about.

"Oh, Keith is all right. He's just a lil' territorial." She said like the old school thug's snobby attitude was nothing. "He feels some kind of way about you coming to work for me. Before you, he was handling security duties for me and Show."

"Fuck that old ass nigga!" Tyson frowned as hot as coals on the grill. "He gon' either bow down to my gangsta or meet with some hot shit."

"Ugh, men," Treasure rolled her eyes.

"Is that your friend?" Tyson asked, peering through the windshield at a slender light skinned girl standing outside of terminal #3. Her hair was done in blonde individual braids. She was small up top, but had an ass shaped like a pumpkin.

THESE SCANDALOUS STREETS

Little momma's attire was an apple jack, Chloe glasses, and a vest over a wife beater. She was standing beside her stack of Louie Vuitton Luggage, talking on her cell and using her shoulder to hold it up to her ear.

"Baby, I'ma call you back, my ride is here. Love you." She kissed at the caller before disconnecting the call.

As soon as the car stopped Treasure hopped out and ran towards her homegirl, arms spread wide open for an embrace. She was coming right at her, sliding her cell phone into her back pocket and spreading open her arms as well. They screamed how women who are friends do when they hadn't seen one another for quite some time.

"I thought that was my bitch!" Treasure screamed.

"Heyyyyy, baby momma!" they collided and hugged lovingly, kissing each other on the cheek.

"Look at chu, girl, looking all fly and shit." Skylar held her at arm's length. "What're those you're rocking, sis?"

"Oh, these old things?" Treasure spoke modestly, glancing down at her boots. "Jimmy Choo's."

"Those are nice. I gotta get me some of those, so I can stunt on those hating ass hoes back home."

Don't trip. I gotchu, momma, we're going shopping on me."

"Oh, I can't wait," she looked to Tyson who was putting her luggage into the trunk of the Maybach. "Well, who is this tall drink of water?"

"Skylar, Tyson. Tyson, this is Skylar, my best girlfriend from back home." Treasure informed him.

"What's up?" Tyson said holding open the door for the ladies to get inside.

"Hey, Chocolate Daddy, I see you got that Morris Chestnut thang going on. Treasure, you didn't tell me you had a new boo thang."

THESE SCANDALOUS STREETS

"Tyson isn't my boo, he's my bodyguard." Treasure blushed but quickly recovered from the expression.

"Oh, well, excuse me. Besides my brother I should have known you didn't have any good taste." Skylar's older brother was Trip, Treasure's late boyfriend.

"Please, let's not get on that lil' buff neck midget you left back in the Bay."

"Whatever. Don't be hating. My nigga is all of that and a bag of hot Cheetos." Skylar claimed as Tyson rolled them out of the LAX airport.

"Where to ladies?" Tyson asked, looking at them through the rearview mirror.

"North Hollywood, we've got some shopping to do." Treasure held up her American Express black card and smacked Skylar five.

***

Treasure and Skylar hit nearly every clothing store in downtown Hollywood, going buck wild with the crooner's black card. They charged everything but a yacht and a G5 jet on it. By the time they were done shopping everyone had five bags in both hands, even Tyson. Treasure was nice enough to cop him a few things. Tyson was thoroughly impressed with her fashion sense. He thought if the singer wasn't a crooner she could have easily been a stylist to stars.

After a long day of shopping the girls decided to go and eat at an oriental restaurant out in Hollywood called Mrs. Lang's. They served everything from Chinese food to Soul Food, and had everything to drink from a can of Sprite to a bottle of Bel Aire. Skylar ordered the Chow Mein noodles, orange chicken and BBQ pork while Treasure opted for the Philly cheese steak, sweet potato French fries and a slice of

THESE SCANDALOUS STREETS

cheese cake. For their drinks, Skylar ordered a glass of water with a slice of lime and Treasure got a Heineken.

Tyson stood at the center of the far west wall keeping an eye out on things, while the girls indulged in their meals and shot the breeze.

"For real? You gotcha own hair salon popping?" Treasure asked with excitement.

"Uh huh, Sky's The Limits," Skylar gave her the name of her hair salon, popping the collar of her vest. "We do manicures and pedicures there, too. You should come and check us out when you touch the turf again. You ain't gotta pay for shit, you know ya bitch gotchu."

"Bet." Treasure dapped her girl up.

After washing her food down with the glass of water, Skylar leaned back in her chair and belched. "Excuse me."

"You'z about a nasty ass bitch," Treasure frowned with disgust, fanning the fumes of the stench. Old girl gave her the middle finger. "Yeah, I know my record is number one on top of the charts." She referred to her holding up the finger before taking a sip of her Heineken.

"I'm fuller than a mug." Skylar patted her stuffed belly. "Can you smoke in here?"

"Not what chu wanna put in the air? This isn't Amsterdam."

"Right," she fished a cigarette from her purse and lit it up, spotting Tyson standing up at a nearby table. "So, what's up with you and Sexual Chocolate over there?" She expelled smoke and nodded to the thugged out bodyguard.

"Ain't nothing up," she glanced over at him and admitted. "Like I told you he's my bodyguard, not my man."

"You mean you aren't tryna hit that?"

THESE SCANDALOUS STREETS

"No, hoe," Treasure laughed, her friend always thought everybody was fucking everybody. "We have a business relationship and that's it."

"It didn't look like that back at the store. Y'all made the cutest lil' couple; you picking out clothes for him and him modeling them for you. Girl, the sales clerk thought that y'all were a couple. She asked me how long had y'all been together."

"Yeah, right."

"Real talk. The chemistry is there, boo boo."

"Skylar, you've been playing make believe since we were five. When are you gonna grow up, babe?"

"Why are you fronting? I know y'all slapping skins."

"I'm sorry to disappoint you, sis, but ain't nothing popping."

"Hooker, the only way it ain't *popping* is if you done gone les'." She eyed her with suspicion.

"Bitch, I'll bust this bottle over your head." she flinched at her with the beer bottle.

"Well, if you haven't made a move then I know he has 'cause he ain't gay. I saw how he was eyeballing you through the rearview." Treasure looked at her like, *for real?* "Uh huh, girl, every time you would look up he would look away."

"He tried, but I shot him down." Treasure confessed, taking a bite of cheese cake. "I told him I don't fuck around with the help."

"Ouch. What a way to bruise a brotha's ego." Skylar said, feeling sorry for good old Tyson. "For you to be turning down dick, you must really be putting that vibrator to work."

Treasure dropped her fork into her plate and it made a clink. She was shocked that her friend made that last statement loud enough for anyone sitting nearby to hear.

THESE SCANDALOUS STREETS

"Oh, my God, Skylar, can you say it any louder? I don't think everybody heard you." The songstress looked over both shoulders to make sure that no one had heard her ghetto ass homegirl. They hadn't.

"My bad, sis, but you do need a lil' dick in your life." She took a sip of water.

Treasure took a swig of her Heineken. If she did get some dick any time soon she wouldn't mind it coming from Tyson.

***

When Treasure and Skylar made it back to Showtime's place they had a slumber party like they did when they were little girls. They painted each other's nails, did one another's hair, gossiped about boys, watched old 80s movies and ate junk food until they puked. The best friends were having a ball until Skylar's boyfriend called. As soon as she'd gotten on the phone she'd forgotten about Treasure.

"Where are you going?" Skylar asked twisting one of her braids around her finger while holding the cell to her ear with her shoulder.

"To make some more popcorn," Treasure answered snobby, rolling her eyes.

"What's wrong with you?" Her brows mushed together, seeing the expression her bestie wore.

"Nothing!" Treasure snapped, closing the door shut on her way out.

Journeying down the hall, she heard the blaring surround sound system in Tyson's bedroom. She could tell he was watching some old martial arts flick from the dialogue and the sound the punches and kicks made when they struck their enemy. Her curiosity got the best of her so she turned around

THESE SCANDALOUS STREETS

and headed toward his bedroom door. She knocked a few times before he finally answered, wearing a wife beater and red corduroy house shoes, which he was walking on the back of.

"My bad, is the TV up too loud?" He asked, pointing over his shoulder with the remote control.

"Nah, its fine, is that The Fist of Fury?"

Tyson looked back at the flat-screen and nodded. "Yep."

"What channel is it on?"

"It's not on TV. I brought a few DVDs while y'all were shopping; I'm having myself a lil' Kung Fu marathon."

"Oh, I love Kung Fu movies." Treasure said excitedly, clapping her hands gently. "You mind if I join you?" she jumped up and down anxiously, hoping that he'd say yes.

"What about cha girl?"

"Her boo called and she's been treating me like a red headed stepchild ever since." She looked up at him awaiting his verdict. There was a moment of silence that changed her mind. "I'm sorry. Look at me intruding on you and you've been bothered with me and my girlfriend all day. I know you probably need a break from us. I'll leave you alone." She headed down the corridor towards the staircase.

"Yo', Treas'," he called after her and she turned around. "Come on." He motioned for her to come into his bedroom.

"Are you sure?" she gave him a look that he read as *It's okay if you say no.*

"Yeah, I'm sure." He gave her that million dollar smile of his. "I hate watching movies by myself. Besides, what good is a Kung Fu marathon without anybody to watch it with? There is a price for admission, though."

Treasure frowned, thinking he was expecting some sexual favor. "What's that?"

"Popcorn."

THESE SCANDALOUS STREETS

"I'm on it." Treasure smiled and skipped down the hallway, toward the staircase.

"Aye, grab me a Coke." Tyson yelled to her, hanging halfway out of the door.

"Alright," She yelled back over her shoulder, descending the steps.

Treasure and Tyson watched Fist of Fury, Shogun Assassins, Five Fingers of Death, White Lotus and Treasure's personal favorite, The Last Dragon. Before long, sleep had invaded them and they drifted off in each other's arms. The scene playing on the flat-screen was of Bruce Leroy and Laura Charles' final kiss.

The singer awoke at the crack of dawn to a static filled flat-screen wiping her eyes. Realizing she was in Tyson's arms she pulled away from him. She stared at him for a while. He was so handsome and looked so peaceful lying there asleep. Smiling, she placed a tender kiss on his cheek and draped a quilt over him. Next, she turned off the flat-screen and made her exit.

Treasure crept back into her bedroom and closed the door gently, careful not to wake Skylar's loud mouth ass up. Approaching the bed she found her friend asleep with her head snuggled up against the pillow. Trying her best not to make so much as a peep, she slid in bed beside her and turned over on her side. She closed her eyes and sighed with relief that she didn't awake.

"So, did homeboy lay it down or what?" Skylar spoke with her eyes closed; she felt that ass creep in.

Treasure laughed and said, "Girl, you are something else, go to sleep."

"Alright, but I want details when I wake up."

"Please, ain't nobody fucking."

"Uh huh, and ain't nobody stupid either."

THESE SCANDALOUS STREETS

Treasure smiled and closed her eyes to go back to sleep. She had dreams of her and Tyson at the altar getting married with a little boy and girl by their side.

THESE SCANDALOUS STREETS

Chapter Ten
Nights later

Romadal's hitters and lieutenants met with some hot shit nearly one after the next. Rock, Tiny, Zitro, Berry and that nigga Loon. The only ones left were Fish and Rodney. Although they knew that their people were dropping like flies they didn't try to play it safe out in the streets. They felt like all they needed were their guns and they were good. In their minds the other guys were stupid and they were smarter so they'd be okay. Besides, they couldn't see themselves staying in on the account that some head busters were after them. Nah, them niggaz had to show face because they were the self-proclaimed Hardest Niggaz in the Streets.

Night fell on the city leaving the moon to reside over South Central Los Angeles. Fish was at Boss Life Customs getting his Envoy truck fitted with 26 inch chrome Giovanni rims.

"Damn, them mu'fuckaz on hit," He stood back looking down at the big boy rims on his SUV, twisting a toothpick at the corner of his mouth.

"Yeah, you gon' be swimmin' in pussy when da hoes see you with deez." A Mexican that worked at the shop by the name of Albert claimed, making sure the nuts of the rim were screwed tight into place on the truck.

"Shiddddd, I'm already drowning in it, homes." He pulled out a fat wad of dead presidents and peeled off a few for the brand new rims. "But, nah, this is for my baby girl. She's graduating tomorrow. You think I can leave it here until tomorrow afternoon? I don't want to ruin the surprise."

Fish had the truck pimped the fuck out. The fellas at Boss Life customs had tricked the SUV out with leather seats, a banging ass stereo system, TVs in the dashboard and

THESE SCANDALOUS STREETS

headrests and wood grain lining on the dashboard and door paneling.

"Sure. Come with me and I'll get your receipt." Albert motioned for him to follow him as he headed for the office to get his change and receipt. "Just let me lock everything up and I'll take care of you, boss." It was closing time so he closed and locked the sliding shutters of the establishment. With Fish in tow, he went around the shop locking the doors and turning out the lights, making sure everything was secure. Once he was done he headed for his office. Stepping over the threshold, he flipped on the light-switch and found his executive chair with its back to him. *Crack!* Crazy whacked him upside the head with his banger, knocking him out cold. He then swung into the doorway, pointing that thang at Fish. The big man slowly lifted his massive hands into the air and allowing the toothpick to dance at the corner of his mouth. His face twisted into a scowl.

"What's up with it?" Crazy quipped.

"'Sup, nigga?" Fish's nostrils flared.

The executive chair slowly spun around revealing Bizeal in its seat. "What's up with it, OG?" He asked with wicked eyes.

"Where that nigga Rodney at?"

Fish stared Crazy down menacingly. His nostrils flared and he clenched his teeth, revealing the skeletal bone structure of his jaw. He didn't pay the husky man in the chair any mind.

"Are you hard of hearing or something?" Bizeal spat angrily, leaning forward in the chair. "Where the fuck is your homeboy?" he stood to his feet with his .45.

Suddenly, Fish spat the toothpick in Crazy's face and cracked him in the jaw, dropping him like a bad habit. He

THESE SCANDALOUS STREETS

darted out of the office, bullets flying over his head as the brute tried to lay him down.

Poc! Poc! Poc!

"Shit!" Bizeal bellowed, punching the desk when he'd missed the throwback hustler. He ran over to his comrade and pulled him to his feet. "Come on." He ran after Fish. Crazy shook off his daze and joined his homeboy in the chase. They chased Fish out of the rim shop, taking shots at him as they went along.

Although he was up in age he was in the physical condition of a man in his prime. He leapt upon the gate of the shop and hopped over with little effort. The young niggaz weren't far behind him though.

"Ughhh!"

"Ughhh!"

Bizeal and Crazy grunted dropping down from over the gate. They spotted Fish running up the block and went after him, pulling the triggers of their burners.

Poc! Poc! Poc!

Bloc! Bloc! Bloc!

The windows of parked cars shattered and sparks flew from the iron-fences of nearby houses when bullets ricocheted off of them.

"Nigga, you can't shoot for shit!" Bizeal spat.

"I don't see you hitting the mothafucka!" Crazy shot back.

"Come on." He told him before running to catch up with Fish.

Fish unlocked the door of his whip. Next, he triggered the door of a secret compartment and withdrew his chrome .9mm. Quickly, he checked its magazine and smacked it back into the bottom of the weapon—*Bwock!* He pulled himself out of the car and came up dumping—*Blac! Blac!*—

THESE SCANDALOUS STREETS

he dropped Crazy with two shots. The young man howled in pain as he went down.

"Aghhh!"

The big man was so busy with Crazy that he neglected giving Bizeal any attention, which he'd soon regret. A hot one through the shoulder dropped him and sent his .9mm skidding underneath his car, nudging it beneath a tire. Fish grimaced as he reached for his piece, feeling the sting of his injury in his shoulder as he bled. Bizeal ran upon him along with Crazy who was cradling his bloody arm.

Bloc! Bloc!

Bizeal's jaws were squared when he squeezed the trigger of his head bussa causing it to jerk violently in his meaty hand. He popped a shot into Fish's leg and thigh. The old school hustler screamed in agony and grabbed for his wounded leg.

"Ahhhh, fuck! My fucking leg, grrrrr!" he bit down hard on his bottom lip, feeling the fire that engulfed his limb.

"Bitch ass nigga!" Bizeal stomped his victim's wounded leg. "That's for making me chase after your old ass."

Crazy stomped his wounded leg, too. "That's for shooting me in my goddamn arm."

"Where's Rodney? I'm not gonna ask you again."

"Fuck y'all! Fuck both of y'all!" Fish bawled on the ground.

"Nah, nigga, fuck you, too!" Bizeal spat. He and Crazy unloaded on Fish. Gunfire roared in the night, sounding like firecrackers, the lights from their muzzles flashing in their faces.

Poc! Bloc! Bloc! Poc! Poc! Poc! Bloc!

Once the shooting ceased there was only blood and gun smoke. The throwback hustler lay still with his eyes staring into space and his mouth ajar. The last thing that went through his head besides a bullet was Master P's song *Is There a Heaven for a Gangsta.*

Bizeal and Crazy took a moment to admire their handiwork, tilting their heads at different angles as they observed their kill like he was a Picasso hanging up inside of an art museum.

Bizeal tucked his warm steel on his waistline and tapped his comrade, saying, "Let's go."

A few nights later

"I can take it from here. You gon' and get your rest, dawg. I'ma settle up with these bitch ass niggaz and show them how we old school cats get down. I'ma put the guns to these young hardheads and make them feel what your wife, your son and your lil' girl are feeling right now. Best believe that, crimey. My word is bond." Rodney swore to Fish-Scale as he stood over his closed casket at his funeral. His bloodshot red eyes rimmed with tears and splashed on the mustard gold casket of his best friend. Fish had gotten shot through the forehead and his dome had swelled up to three times its normal size. His face was left so deformed and mangled that his wife had no choice but to give him a closed casket service. The service was held two weeks ago at Solomon's memorial and Rodney had been taking his grief out on his liver ever since.

Rodney sat at the bar in The Bar Fly hunched over a glass of Jack Daniel's. It was his 5th glass straight of the dark liquor and he showed no signs of slowing down. The alcohol had the kick of a donkey, but its affects were desperately needed. He required it to suppress the sorrow behind his best friend's death. He didn't know in his who killed Fish but he wouldn't rest until his murder was avenged. Once he was

THESE SCANDALOUS STREETS

done sulking and drinking himself into oblivion he was going to load up his guns and gather his troops. Together they'd scour the streets for his homeboy's executioner, and once they found him he was going to be the one to put the bullet in his head that cancelled his subscription to life.

Rodney stared at the glass of Jack with glassy, bloodshot eyes. He swallowed what was left of it and smacked the glass down on the bar. He motioned the bartender over to refill his glass. A slender old man with a crown of kinky gray hair wrung out the towel he'd used to wipe the bar down and slung it over his shoulder. He grabbed the bottle of Jack Daniel's from behind the bar and approached his regular patron. He noticed the pain written on the man's face as he refilled his glass.

"Shit, Rod, you look like somebody kicked your dog." He commented on his expression.

"Worse." He replied picking up his glass of Jack. "Niggaz took my right hand."

The bartender thought on who he could be talking about. He'd seen him come through the bar with quite a few heads, but there was one cat he saw him with more often than the others. "You mean, Fish?" the bartender asked with furrowed brows. "The tall, built cat that used to come in here with you every Thursday night shooting pool and talking shit?" Rodney nodded yes. "Man, I sure hate to hear that. He was a cool brother; real good peoples."

"That he was." Rodney agreed before taking a sip of his drink. About forty minutes later, he was paying for his drinks and dropping the bartender a healthy tip.

"You outta here?" the bartender asked, scooping up the bills.

THESE SCANDALOUS STREETS

Rodney threw up two fingers as he stood to his feet. He wanted to leave but his legs felt like noodles under him and he went spilling to the floor, knocking over stools.

"You all right?" the bartender asked, helping him to his feet.

"Yeah, I'm straight. I might need a lil' help to my car, though." He slurred.

"You've gotta be jiving me. Nigga, sit your ass down," the bartender pushed him back down onto the stool. "I'm calling you a cab." He turned to Rodney after calling up the cab. "Your ride will be here in ten minutes."

"Thanks, Nigel," he thanked him before whipping out a Zippo lighter and lighting a Black & Mild. He took a drag and expelled smoke from his nostrils and mouth. He looked over the patrons: some were sitting at the tables drinking and conversing, while others stood around watching a couple of cats shoot pool. There were some sprinkled throughout the establishment talking and taking swigs of cold ones as well.

Rodney scratched his temple with his thumb and turned around on his stool to Nigel. "Say, man, I'ma head on over to this store at the corner here and get myself a couple packs of Excedrin. I know I'ma have the mother of all headaches in the morning."

"Alright, but fork over your car keys."

Rodney smiled drunkenly. "So what, you don't believe me?"

"Hell naw." Nigel snapped his fingers and motioned for the car keys.

Rodney stood to his feet laughing. He dug into his pocket and tossed Nigel his keys.

***

THESE SCANDALOUS STREETS

Rodney staggered out of the corner store with a brown paper bag. In addition to the packs of Excedrin, he got a pack of Swishers, a 5th of Gin and a little bottle of orange juice. Making his way back toward The Bar Fly, he took the half of the Black & Mild from behind his ear and relit it. He took a pull and blew a gust of smoke into the air. He walked along without a care in the world, until the crackling of gravel at his rear gave him cause to look back. A car with its headlights out trailed behind him beside the curb. His stomach twisted into knots when he saw the car approaching. The presence of death hovered in the air like a foul stench, causing him to sober up quick. He turned back around pretending not to have noticed the car. He eased the Beretta from his waistline and slowed his stroll, allowing the car to get close enough for him to take advantage. In one swift motion, he dropped his bag of goods and spun around, pumping round after round through the windshield of the car where the driver sat.

Boc! Boc! Boc! Boc! Boc!

The windshield cracked into several spider's webs. The car jumped the curb and crashed into a light post, scrunching its hood. Gun at his side, Rodney approached the car with caution. The closer he drew in the more visible the car became. It was a yellow Crown Victoria taxi. Rodney peered inside the taxi and saw a Palestinian man, sitting slumped in the driver seat. He reached in and leaned the man's head back. His eyes were rolled to their whites and his mouth was open.

"Aaahhhh!" He expelled his last breath. Rodney looked down to his chest. It was stained crimson and plagued with gaping holes, some of which squirted blood.

"Goddamn!" Rodney pounded the roof of the taxi, hating to have killed an innocent man. He brought his hand down

THESE SCANDALOUS STREETS

his face and when he looked up the night began to stir. People were coming out of The Bar Fly, a nearby nightclub, as well as the corner store, to see what had happened. He heard police car sirens as well as a police helicopter coming from a far, so he knew someone had already called 911. Scooping up his brown bag of goods, Rodney broke down the alleyway.

***

    Rodney entered his home, slamming the door behind him. He tossed his bag of goods on the coffee table and headed into the kitchen, where he peered through the blinds of the window residing over the sink, looking for the helicopter that he was sure followed him home. His eyes searched the sky until they found the police helicopter. He watched it attentively as it soared over his house and out of his neighborhood.
    Rodney ducked into the bathroom and plugged the sink. He stood on top of the commode and urinated in it. He removed his shirt and thoroughly washed his hands in the golden bath; cleansing his mitts of the gunpowder that stained his hands when he's discharged the Beretta. Once he was done he rewashed his hands with soap and dried them off on a bath towel that hung on the bar of the sliding shower door. After stashing the rest of the guns and drugs he kept in the house, he punched a number into his cell and held it to his ear. Walking back into the kitchen he took another peek through the blinds to see if the helicopter had truly left. It was gone.
    "Hello," he said into the cellular as he walked back into the living room. "Nigel, what the hell happened down there, man? I came outta the store and the next thing I hear is

THESE SCANDALOUS STREETS

gunshots. Damn, for real? Shit, I don't know. Once I heard them shots I sobered up real quick and got the fuck outta dodge. Nah, I'm alright. Okay. You be careful out there, man. I'll come by there and check you tomorrow. Peace." He disconnected the call and sat the phone on the kitchen counter. He put his hands on his hips and thought about what just happened minutes ago. "What the fuck is wrong with me? This young nigga got me paranoid, killing innocent mothafuckaz. He got me off my square. I'ma have to tighten homes up, pronto." He shook his head shamefully.

Rodney felt a cool breeze that caused him to shiver; he headed down the hall into his bedroom, where he found the window cracked open. He shook his head and said, "This bitch Yuriko. I tell that broad all the time to lock my shit up when she comes through here." He closed the window and locked the latch.

Rodney picked up his bag from the coffee table before heading into the kitchen. He dropped a handful of ice into a glass and filled it half way with Gin and orange juice. After stirring the alcohol beverage with a spoon, he raised the glass to take a sip. That's when he saw the distorted image of someone behind him through the glass of the kitchen window over the sink.

"Haaa!" He gasped, eyes widening with fear and before he knew it a plastic bag was pulled over his face. Putting up a fight for his life, he dropped his glass and it shattered on the floor, leaving Gin and shards everywhere. He kicked and thrashed around violently, knocking over dishes and chairs. He blindly tried to gouge his assailant's eyes out, but to no avail. The struggle he was putting up proved to be futile, since lack of oxygen had left him in a weakened state. In one last attempt he grabbed for the Beretta on his waistline but came up with air. At that moment it dawned on him that he'd

THESE SCANDALOUS STREETS

ditched it in the dumpster inside the alley in case the police would be on his trail after murking the cab driver. *Damn!*

"Night, night, nigga," the assailant said through clenched jaws as sweat dripped from his brow. Rodney's struggling grew weaker and weaker until all together his movements ceased. He went slack in his killer's arms.

Thud!

The little big head nigga sounded like a slab of ribs hitting the floor. Looking down at his lifeless form, the killa whipped out a bandana from his back pocket and wiped his forehead. He left through the back door and hopped the fence where Bizeal awaited him in the alley.

"That nigga done?" the husky man inquired, driving off.

"Finito." Malakai wiped the sweat from his forehead with the back of his hand. He pulled a small tablet from his back pocket and flipped it open. He took a pen from the console and crossed out the first to last name on his hit list *Rodney*. The Sheridan complex was almost his.

Rodney lay dead in the middle of his kitchen floor. He died knowing he'd broken his word to his dearest friend and that to him was worse than death.

THESE SCANDALOUS STREETS

Chapter Eleven

"Where are y'all headed?" Showtime asked as he walked into the kitchen in his swimming trunks dripping wet. He opened his subzero refrigerator and rummaged around inside.

"Dreamland; I gotta appearance there tonight." Treasure responded from where she stood beside Skylar and Tyson. "If you wanna come we can wait."

"I'll have to take a rain check," he took a few champagne flutes from the cupboard, wedging them between his fingers. He'd already gotten the bottle of Belaire from out of the refrigerator. "As you can see, me and fellas have guests." He nodded towards the glass double doors that lead to the outside, where Dead Beat and Keith was in the Jacuzzi with three bikini clad Brazilians. The tanned vixens could barely speak English but they were finer than wine. It looked like a Playboy swimsuit issue was being shot outside.

"Oh, alright." Treasure replied.

"Tyson, you make sure you take care of my girl now." The CEO of Big Willie records told his newest employee as he headed through the glass doors.

"No doubt," Tyson replied. He held out his arms for the girls to grab a hold of and they obliged. "Ladies shall we?" he looked to each one of the visions on his arm with a smile.

"Yes, we shall." They replied in unison.

***

When Tyson and the girls arrived at club Dreamland there were throngs of people waiting behind the velvet rope to get inside. You would have thought they were waiting in

THESE SCANDALOUS STREETS

line for the midnight release of the new Michael Jordan sneaker. Men and women were out in their best; smelling good and looking good. Some chicks rocked the authentic clothes and bags from Gucci, Louie Vuiton, D&G and Prada, while others were in knock-offs they brought from old boy that came through the salons they got their hair and nails done at.

The fellas were fly too. Some of them had on the real brands of European designers while the rest sported fugazi clothes and sneakers from the trunk of some bootlegger's car. All in all, everyone had left their problems at home and had come out to have themselves a good time.

Tyson and the girls made their way past the people waiting in line receiving glares and whispers from them.

"Look at these bitches."

"They aren't all of that."

"Oh, shit. That's Treasure Gold."

"Fool, that ain't Treasure."

"The hell it ain't."

"Bitch that is her!"

The crowd erupted into pandemonium and everyone rushed in trying to get a glimpse of the superstar crooner and get her autograph. The bouncers held them off until Tyson and the girls were secure inside of the club.

Tyson held Treasure's hand and she held Skylar's as he made his way through the maze of bodies that massed the dance floor. He took them over to the VIP section, where they sat on a black suede couch. A hostess with a long silky ponytail that hung passed her "50 inch ass sashayed over with a bucket of Ace of Spade on ice and two champagne flutes. She had an average face but was as thick as Skippy peanut butter. After sitting the bucket and flutes on the table

THESE SCANDALOUS STREETS

she said, "Hi, I'm Nicole. I'll be your host for the night. If you need anything else be sure to let me know."

"Here you go, Nicole." Treasure handed her a crisp Benjamin.

"Thank you." She took the bill with a grateful smile.

"You're welcome, sweetie."

"Man, that's a huge broad." Skylar commented once Nicole had gone, eyes lingering on her. She watched as she walked away, her long ponytail swinging from left to right. "I wouldn't even fight her; I'd shoot her big ass."

Treasure laughed as she filled their flutes with champagne. She handed her best friend one while she kept the other. "Here's to the good life." She held up her flute.

"The good life," Skylar touched her flute into her home girl's in a toast before they both took a sip. "It's live in here tonight." She looked over the sea of people dancing out on the floor; they were moving to the sounds of the beat and wearing jovial expressions. The club's music was so loud that waves formed in the champagne in their glasses. Skylar leaned over to Treasure and asked, "Girl, how much are they paying you for this gig?"

"$100,000."

"Damn. You don't even have to perform? Just sit here and look pretty?"

"And sip champagne." She smiled wickedly like she was doing something evil before taking a sip of bubbly.

"My baby momma doing the damn thang," Skylar gave her girl a high five.

"Thanks, boo."

Skylar went on yapping but Treasure was only half listening. See at the moment someone else had her attention and his name was Tyson McGowan. He stood outside of the velvet rope of the VIP section, fitted in a black suede blazer, which he wore over a black V-neck. At the moment he chewed on Winter Fresh gum wearing a dead serious look while on the job. His head was on a swivel as he surveyed the atmosphere of the club.

A smile broadened Treasure's face as she stared at him. She knew he was a street nigga and at first she thought he was like the rest of the cats she knew back home. But the night she'd spent with him had changed that for her. From that night forth she knew that he was different from any other man she'd dealt with. There was something about him that made him special. She couldn't quite put her finger on it, but whatever it is was drawing her to him.

Treasure snapped back to reality once Skylar stepped into her line of vision with her hands on her hips. She looked up and she was smiling at her.

"You got it bad, sis. Old boy got chu open like a jar of jelly."

"What? Please." She frowned and waved her off.

Skylar sat back down beside her. "He really got chu jonesin, huh? That must have been one hell of a night you two had."

"I'm not Jonesin. The boy's only been here about a week. And like I told you before, *'Nothing happened between us.'* All we did was watch Kung fu flicks."

"Well, you said you fell asleep in his arms right? I know how much you like to cuddle after getting your back blown out." She smirked with a knowing look.

"True. But we didn't have sex." Treasure assured her. "And me falling asleep in his arms was by accident."

"Uh huh." Skylar gave her a *Yeah, right* look. "Well, the look you were giving him doesn't lie. I remember when you use to look at my brother like that." Tears welling up in her eyes.

THESE SCANDALOUS STREETS

"Aww, come here, Sky." The R & B sensation hugged her best friend and pecked her on top of the forehead. "There isn't any man on earth that can replace Trip in my heart."

"I know." She wiped the tears from her face. "'Cause even in death my brother has a hold on you, but chu gotta let him go, Treas. You gotta let him go and allow yourself to fall in love again. It's what he would have wanted. Trust me. I knew Zo like no other."

"I know, girl." Treasure nodded as she wiped the tears from the corners of her eyes.

"Y'all alright?" Tyson asked from behind the velvet rope, a look on concern written across her face.

"Yeah, we're good." Skylar assured him, throwing her arm over her girl's shoulder and pulling her close. Tilting her head down, she said something into her ear that caused her to smile and giggle. She then kissed her on the side of her head in a show of sisterly affection.

Right then, French Montana's *Pop That* flooded the club and patrons abandoned their drinks to hit the dance floor. Skylar downed the last of her champagne like it was a shot of Whiskey and grabbed Treasure's hand.

"Come on, Treas. This is my song." She led her out on the dance floor, flailing her hand in the air and snapping her fingers.

Meanwhile

Bo sat at the bar throwing back shots of Jose Cuervo like they were water. He and his boys watched Treasure and Skylar on the dance floor with glassy lustful eyes. The alcohol mixed with the cocaine in his system played tricks with his mental. He believed he saw the girls on the dance floor sexing each other, butt ass naked.

THESE SCANDALOUS STREETS

"Them bitches bad." Skooter commented before throwing back another shot.

"Ain't that the singer broad? What's here name?" Marlon asked, massaging his chin, moving his head about for a better look. He was a thin, big head nigga with a receding hairline.

"Treasure Gold," Bo told him not having taken his eyes off the crooner and her friend. He was a bald head dude with a muscular build.

"Yeah, that's her, Treasure." Marlon slid his tongue around inside of his mouth, eying the songstress like he was a hungry dog and she was a T-bone steak. The singer's body was off the mothafucking chain to him.

"I'd eat the shit out of that pussy. On momma, I'd beat them shits raw and the whole nine." Skooter grabbed the bulge in his pants.

"I'm sure you would, Skooter," Bo threw back a shot. "But while y'all sit here drooling over the bitch like she's some Playboy pinup, I'ma slide over there and lay down my spiel, you feel me?" he sat the glass down and motioned the bartender over to refill his drink. The bartender refilled his glass and he paid for his tab. "There you go." He dropped a couple of dead white men onto the bar top then stuffed his wad of bills into his pocket.

"Yeah, gone and get all liquored up so you can deal with the rejection when homegirl shoots you down." Skooter made his hand into the shape of a gun and pointed it at Bo saying, "Pow! Pow! Pow! Pow!" he blew imaginary smoke from his index finger and smiled. Marlon busted up laughing.

"Chuck it up now, ladies, 'cause tonight I'll be home in some warm pussy while y'all fools will be laid up with your dick in your hand." Bo threw back his last shot and rose to his feet, straightening out the wrinkles in his white suit. He slicked the imaginary loose hairs down on the sides of his head and held his palm out before his mouth, blowing his hot breath in it. The repugnant stench caused him to frown and flinch. After spraying his mouth with Banocka, he stashed the small tube away and checked his breath again. Satisfied, he went about his business of procuring those digits. His boys laughed at him as he drunkenly staggered out on the dance floor.

Bo made his way through the people gathered out on the dance floor while en route in Treasure and Skylar's direction. He ended up bumping shoulders with a cat dancing with his lady and fell to the floor. The man tried to help him back upon his feet but he breathed fire into his face and shoved him back.

"Fuck is yo' problem, man?" the cat grimaced as his lady held to his arm, having just stopped him from falling.

"You're my problem bitch," he breathed fire. "And if you keep it up you gon' be the coroners problem in a minute." He and old boy mad dogged one another for a time until his lady decided to intervene.

"Come on, baby, just forget about him. Let's have a good time." She started back grinding up on her man. When she saw that Bo still had his attention, she placed his hands on her hips and ground harder into him. That got his undivided attention.

"Punk ass nigga." Bo set his sights back on Treasure wearing a confident expression and rubbing his hands together, as he approached. He cleared his throat. "Excuse me, beautiful, but may I have this dance?"

Treasure didn't hear his muscle head ass over the loud music not to mention she was engrossed in dancing with Skylar to even notice him. Once again he cleared his throat

THESE SCANDALOUS STREETS

and repeated himself, but she still didn't hear him. The nigga felt like she was trying to play him like he was some kind of bum ass nigga and that enraged him. He grabbed her roughly by her arm and pulled her into him. He stared Treasure in the face with madness in his eyes, breathing heavily in her face and resembling a raging bull. She could smell the combination of alcohol and cigarettes on his breath.

"Bitch, you gotta lil' paper now yo' ass den went Hollywood? Fuck you think you are? Tryna play a nigga to the left like you're the only one out here getting money. I'm Big Bo from 107, ask around." He pulled a stack of cash from his suit that was telephone book thick and threw it in her face. *Swhack!* The bills smacked up against her and went flying everywhere, scattering as they fell to the dance floor.

"Oh, no in the fuck you didn't," Skylar snarled and cracked the mammoth of a man in the mouth. The blow staggered him but it wasn't enough to drop him. He touched his lips and his fingers came away with blood. The muscle headed man sneered exposing his blood stained teeth. Right after, he held back his hand and uncoiled a vicious backhand slap that spun the petite woman around and sent her crashing to the floor. She lay there holding her stinging cheek.

"Are you okay?" Treasure kneeled to her friend.

"Yeah," Skylar winced.

Treasure's head snapped in Bo's direction. She looked at him like he made the biggest mistake of his life. "You bastard!" she bellowed, swinging wildly on him. He grabbed her by her wrist and cocked his fist back. He moved to punch her lights out and that's when a strong hand grasped his wrist, squeezing it tightly. *Crack!* He heard his wrist bone crackling under the intense pressure.

"Arghhhhh!" The mammoth howled in pain as the vice like grip began to crush his wrist bone as he was turned him

THESE SCANDALOUS STREETS

around to face his aggressor. The 180 degree turn left him face to face with the menacing glare of Tyson. His eyebrows were arched, his nose was scrunched and his jaws were squared so tightly that they pulsated. He resembled a lion assuming the position to pounce on his prey.

"You bitch made ass nigga, hitting on females!" The thug sneered. He grabbed Bo by the collar and slammed his forehead into his nose and mouth. *Bockk!* The blow sounded on impact, breaking both bone and teeth. The brutal assault sent a river of blood spilling down his chin and staining his suit.

"Awww, fuck! My nose, man! My mothafucking nose!" Bo cupped his spurting nose with both hands. Blood seeped through between his fingers and he dropped to his knees. Tyson finished him off with a sharp spin kick to the skull that sent him slamming into the floor.

Thud!

By this time the music had stopped and the lights had come on in the club. The patrons had formed a circle around Tyson and the girls. Tyson went to check on the girls and grimaced when fire shot through his arm.

"Arrhhh!" His head snapped to his wounded arm and he clutched it. Looking up, he saw Skooter with a broken Heineken bottle; its jagged edges twinkled under the lighting, trickling with blood. The nigga lunged at him a few times but he easily dodged his advances. The two men circled each other and when he lunged again, he grabbed him by the arm. He twisted his wrist causing him to drop the broken beer bottle and broke his arm over his shoulder. *Snappp!* There was a sickening pop as Skooter's forearm bone broke and stabbed through his skin, bloody. He screamed in agony. "Rahhhhh!" Tyson grabbed him by the

THESE SCANDALOUS STREETS

back of his neck and slammed his face through a table. *Thoomp!* He heard it break in half.

"Tyson, watch out!" Treasure yelled as loud as she could, veins forming in her neck and temples.

Tyson spun out of the way just as Marlon tried to tackle him. He snatched up a chair while in motion and swung it back around, breaking it over his back. *Brockkk!* The young man went spilling to the floor and bumping his head. Skylar frowned and stomped him in the balls.

"Ahhhhhhh!" He howled in pain but a sharp kick across the jaw left him unconscious.

"Punk ass nigga," She spat on him, the goo splattered against the side of his face.

"Fuck is going on here?"

A gruff voice came from everyone's rear. They turned around and saw two hulking bouncers running in their direction.

"Now, y'all niggaz show up?"Tyson, clutched his bleeding arm.

"Everyone get the hell out of the way." A different voice commanded with authority.

Tyson looked over his shoulder and saw two of Killah Cali's finest making their way through the crowd. "Ladies it's time to boogie." he took Treasure's hand and she took Skylar's, together they ran to the back of the club towards the backdoor exit. With a powerful kick the door went flying open into the crisp cold air. Tyson and the girls spilled out into the alley. He looked both ways before leading them to where he'd parked the car, their shoes trampling over loose trash and broken glass.

***

THESE SCANDALOUS STREETS

Skylar drove the Maybach while Treasure sat in the backseat tending to Tyson's wounded arm.

"Tyson, this looks bad, we're gonna have to get you to the hospital." She informed him after examining his arm.

"Nah, fuck the 'spital, I hate them." He winced, looking to his injury.

"Alright, okay. I think I can stitch you up."

"Cool." He leaned his head back against the headrest. Treasure removed her blouse and tied it around his arm.

Skylar was driving so fast that she hit a pothole that nearly caused Tyson and Treasure's heads to hit the ceiling.

"Yo, slim," Tyson hollered up front to her, smacking the headrest of the front passenger seat. "Slow this mothafucka down! I'm not tryna get knocked with these burners in here!" he spoke of the .45 automatics stashed underneath the passenger seat.

"I'm tryna get chu to King." She looked up at him through the rearview mirror.

"We're not going to the hospital, sis, take it home. I can patch this up."

"I-Yi-Captain," little momma adjusted the rearview mirror. She watched as her best friend interlocked her fingers with her bodyguard and leaned her head against his shoulder, resting her eyes on the rest of the ride home. Tyson leaned his head on top of hers and closed his eyes, too.

Skylar smiled.

THESE SCANDALOUS STREETS

Chapter Twelve

Tyson sat on the end of his bed stitching up his wounds with a needle and thread. Treasure sat beside him holding the first-aid kit, watching him attentively. "Here, let me," she said seeing him having difficulty sewing up the gashes in his arm. She sat the first-aid kit on the bed and bent her knees down to the carpet. Next, she took the needle and thread from him and continued to sew up his arm. *Knock! Knock! Knock!* Someone tapped at the door.

"Yeah?" Tyson yelled over his shoulder.

"It's Sky. Can I come in?" her voice boomed from the other side of the door.

"Come on, slim." He replied.

Skylar came inside smiling. "I hope I'm not interrupting anything."

"Nah, me and your girl are just playing doctor."

She pecked Tyson on the cheek and he blushed with a look of surprise on his face. "What's that for?"

"Just me saying thank you for having our backs tonight."

"That's what they pay me for."

"I know…but still…thanks."

"You're welcome."

There was an uncomfortable silence until she spoke again.

"Well, I guess I'll return to my room and wait for my boo to call me back. Goodnight y'all." She waved as she headed out of the bedroom.

"Goodnight." Tyson said back. Once the door clicked closed he looked to Treasure. "That was sweet of her."

"Yeah, Skylar is tough and ghetto as all hell, but underneath all that gangsta she's a sweetheart." Treasure informed him. "That's my girl."

THESE SCANDALOUS STREETS

"Hey, you're pretty good at this." He referred to her expertise stitching skills. "Let me find out you were a nurse before this singing shit."

"Nah, I use to do my friends hair back in high school. Same method as sewing in weaves."

They laughed.

"Don't laugh at me."

Suddenly, their eyes met. He took a serious expression while she kept her smile, looking down shyly. She focused her attention back on her stitching up his gashes.

"You have a beauty smile."

She blushed. "Thought you said I wouldn't know when you're running game?"

Tyson tilted her chin with his curled finger so she'd be looking him into his soft brown eyes. "This isn't game. This is real spit."

"Is that right?"

"True story."

Treasure's mouth met Tyson's and their tongues did a dance before they locked lips in a passionate, steamy kiss. As their mouths massaged one another's, she pushed him back onto the bed and straddled him. She pulled off her shirt and helped him remove his wife beater. He grimaced as he brought the undershirt from over his head; its removal brought forth the pain of his wound.

"I'm sorry. Are you okay?" Treasure asked concerned.

"Yeah, I'm fine." Tyson smiled. "I'm made of steel. I'm from The Bottoms, baby. We're built to last."

She leaned forward to kiss him and someone rapped on the door.

"Shit!" she cursed and hopped off of him, grabbing her shirt.

THESE SCANDALOUS STREETS

"Who is it?" Tyson called out, putting his wife beater back on.

"It's Showtime." He spoke in a game show host kind of voice.

"Its open." He responded, trying to look natural beside Treasure.

Showtime opened the door and came into the bedroom. "What's up, family? Skylar told me about what happened at Dreamland, are y'all okay?"

"We're solid. Your girl's taking care of me." Tyson looked to his sewn up arm.

"Not bad." The multimillionaire inspected the stitches in his arm. "I got some painkillers if you want a couple."

"Cool."

"Alright. I'll have Preston bring them to you." Showtime addressed Treasure. "Are you still going to see your pops in the A.M?"

"Yeah."

"Well, I'll have Keith procure a rental."

"Alright."

"Good night y'all," Showtime gave his parting words as he closed the door behind him.

Treasure locked the door behind Showtime and straddled Tyson, continuing their make out session. Raising his back from the bed, he helped her remove her shirt. He placed soft kisses down her neck onto her collarbone. Cupping her left breast, he worked his way down and that's when he discovered the ink on her bosom. It was three hearts wrapped in a vine with thorns that read: *R.I.P Trip.*

Tyson stopped and looked up at Treasure. She looked from him to the tattoo and then back again. She then crawled off of him and put her shirt back on. He sat up in bed looking at her with furrowed brows.

THESE SCANDALOUS STREETS

"Treas, what's up? Did I do something wrong?"

"Goodnight." She left his bedroom, closing the door shut behind her.

Tyson fell back on the bed looking dumbfounded; he exhaled and closed his eyes.

The next morning he got dressed and loaded up his twin .45s. He walked across the hall to Treasure's bedroom to see if she was ready to leave. He knocked on the door before entering.

Knock! Knock! Knock!

"Who is it?" Skylar asked from the other side of the door.

"Tyson."

"Oh, it's your boo, Treas." He heard Skylar say before she opened the door.

Skylar pulled open the door holding her cell phone to her ear. Tyson asked her where her homegirl was and she pointed to the bathroom. He headed into the bathroom and found the woman he was assigned to protect in the mirror putting on makeup.

"What's up?" he asked.

"What's up?" she stayed focused on her reflection, applying eyeliner.

"Are you almost ready?"

"Yeah, in a sec, I'm almost done."

"Alright," He looked around the bathroom trying to figure out how to come at her about last night.

"Listen," he began, closing the door for privacy. "I think we should talk about last night."

"What about last night?" she played ignorant.

"What almost went down between us; we were getting hot and heavy and all of a sudden you just up and left when you caught me staring at your tattoo. Who is Trip anyway, a relative or a boyfriend that passed away?" Lines creased his forehead.

Treasure put the cap on her eyeliner and turned around. "Look, Tyson, I don't appreciate you tryna get all up in my mix. It's unprofessional. Me and you have a boss and employee type of relationship and that's how it needs to stay." She moved her neck like an irate hood rat straight out of projects, one French tip manicured hand on her hip.

Tyson looked at Treasure sideways like *Oh, so it's like that now, huh?* "All right, Ms. Gold. I'll be waiting downstairs when you and your guest are ready." He replied with a frown, temples pulsating.

"Thank you, Mr. McGowan." Treasure turned back around to the mirror to finish applying her makeup.

Fifteen minutes later the gang was on the road with Tyson behind the wheel, glancing occasionally into the rearview mirror at the woman he was hired to protect. Treasure and Skylar played the backseat whispering amongst one another. The singer caught him eyeballing her but she didn't pay him any mind. In fact sometimes she would roll her eyes at him.

"What happened between you and Ty back at Showtime's?" Skylar asked her friend in a hushed tone. She'd noticed during the ride that her girl and her bodyguard hadn't shared much dialogue. So she figured something must have gone down between them.

"We ended up kissing last night and we almost…"

"Ohhh," Skylar cupped her hands over her mouth. She didn't even let Treasure finish what she was saying. Uh uh, she was ready to hear some juicy gossip. "Girlllll, tell me what happened?"

"There isn't much to tell. We were making out, our clothes came off. I realized what was about to happen and I stopped him." She admitted nonchalantly as she flipped through an issue of Italian Vogue.

"Scandalous." Skylar concurred. "How you gonna give a brotha the winning ticket to a million dollar lottery and then snatch it back? Bitch, you know you ain't right. Treasure Gold, your heart has the chill of a Chicago winter."

Treasure glanced up and locked eyes with Tyson through the rearview mirror. They held one another's gazes for a time before lowering their eyes. While the girls hit any and every store in the Cerritos malls, Tyson played the background watching over them like a guardian angel. He wore a hard face and kept his arms folded across his chest. His presence was one that said *Don't fuck with me right now because I'm on one.* Occasionally Treasure would glance over at him taking notice of his demeanor. She felt kind of bad being as how she lead him on, but knew now wasn't the time to apologize.

After grabbing a bite to eat at Fat Burgers, they shot back to the mansion and pigged out. They watched TV and shot the shit the rest of the night. Treasure found herself glancing at the staircase wondering if Tyson was going to ever come down to join them but he never did. It was about 6:30 PM when the girls had decided to retire to their bedrooms.

"Night, Treas." Skylar hugged her sister from another mister.

"Night, Sky." Treasure replied. "I love you."

"I love you, too." she kissed her on the cheek.

Treasure waited inside of the hallway until Skylar had entered her bedroom and closed the door shut. She moved to go inside of her own bedroom when a thought entered her mind. As quietly as a cat burglar, she crept over to Tyson's bedroom door and pressed her ear up against it, listening to it. She lifted her fist to knock so she could finally apologize to him, but something stayed her hand.

He's probably in there knocked out, I'll tell him in the morning, She dropped her hand beside her and carried herself across the threshold into her bedroom, closing the door.

Knock! Knock! Knock!

Treasure frowned when she heard someone rapping at the door having just closed it shut. She turned around in time to see a golden envelope being pushing underneath the door. Curious, she picked it up and quickly unlocked the door, pulling it open. Her head was on a swivel as she searched up and down the hallway, looking for the deliverer of the envelope. Not seeing anyone in sight, she closed and locked the door back. Thereafter, she was opening the envelope and pulling out the card. She flipped it open and read what was scrolled across it.

Meet me for dinner tonight at 8 o'clock. I'm not taking no for an answer. Tyson.

A smiled stretched across Treasure's face as she studied the message twisting a nail at the corner of her teeth. She had planned on easing herself in a hot bath and sipping some Moscato for the remainder of the night, but a night out on the town sounded more alluring. Besides, she found Tyson dark and mysterious. She wanted to know more about him. She didn't know what it was about him that drew her in like a magnet to a refrigerator but she was dying to find out.

What the hell. I think I've gotta lil' something, something I've been dying to wear, Treasure tossed the envelope and card on the nightstand and moved for the closet. She swept through each hanging hanger until she found the dress she was looking for. *Bingo!* The songstress smiled and sucked her teeth, sliding her tongue along the inside of her mouth. A gracious expression was plastered across her face as she laid a navy blue and nude Tadashi Shoji cap sleeve lace gown with a flower print on it upon the bed. She hurried back over to the closet and took down a shoe box, removing the lid. Inside there was a simple pair of navy blue high heel pumps that she'd never worn. After picking the pumps out of the box and sitting them on top of the dress, she hopped up from off of the bed. Placing her hands on her hips, she angled her head, taking a good look at the dress and matching heels.

"Ooooooh, I'm finna kill 'em tonight." Treasure smiled happily and swung on the air. She gathered everything she needed to take care of her hygiene and ducked off into the bathroom. An hour later singer was sitting on the edge of the bed oiling her arms, body, and legs. Next, she sprayed on some Beyonce Pulse perfume and styled her hair in a Chinese mane. After that there was the pearl earrings and necklace which she wore over the dress. She slid on the pumps, her pearl bracelet, and matching pinky ring. She gave herself the once over in the Vanity mirror before grabbing her handbag.

Knock! Knock! Knock! Knock!

"That's him." She jumped up antsy and excitedly. Calm down bitch, get a grip. *Don't let this nigga see you drooling all over him like you thirsty and shit.* She stole a glance through the mirror again, fixing her mane and straightening out her dress. After taking a deep breath, she approached the door and turned the knob, pulling it open. Treasure was mesmerized by a snazzy dressed Tyson. He'd given himself a shape up before he stepped out on the scene so his hairline and goatee were on point. He looked like he'd just came from a magazine shoot in his plaid shirt and tie which he wore under a red Polo sweater vest. His Levi's 501 jeans were starched and crisp, so much so that they looked like they could stand up on their own. They went perfectly with his low top red All Star Chuck Taylor Converses. And so were the accessories that were accompanying him. His gold wire rim glasses decorated his face and the plain faced Rolex watch on his wrist made him appear grown and sophisticated. When his lips curled at their ends dimples accented his cheeks and gave birth to a million dollar smile.

Damn, baby is fahhhhine, Treasure feasted her eyes upon him, biting down on the corner of her bottom lip. She was pleased with the chocolate eye candy before her. Her jaw damn near hit the floor, until she pulled herself back together. She couldn't let him see that she was feeling him like crazy so she cleared her throat and straightened up.

"Hey," Treasure tried her best to contain her blushing and smiling. She looked down at the floor then back up into his hypnotizing soft brown eyes.

"What's up, beautiful? Is that for me?" he asked, eyes focused near her ear.

She swept her manicured hand through her hair on the side of her head. Frowning, she said, "What?"

"This."

As if by magic he pulled a long stemmed red rose from behind her ear, presented to her. Wow was written across her face when she saw him do this. "Oh my God, but how did you..."

"Shhhhh!" he held a crooked finger to his lips. "Can you keep a secret?"

"Nahhh." She shook her head as she took the rose from him, closing her eyes and inhaling the scent.

"Neither can I so I may as well tell you now that our ride is downstairs." He offered his arm and she hooked hers

THESE SCANDALOUS STREETS

within his. After closing the door behind her, she allowed her date to lead her to their destination.

As soon as Tyson and Treasure crossed the threshold to the outside they found two horses and a carriage awaiting them. Its driver was a stoic white man with a neatly trimmed mustache and beard that aligned his jaw line perfectly. He was dressed in a charcoal apple jack and matching suit which he wore under an overcoat. Seeing the couple approaching, he tipped his hat and opened the door to the carriage smiling. Treasure smiled from ear to ear when she saw the seasoned gentleman and their ride for the night. She looked amazed. Her eyes snapped open and she mouthed *Wow,* looking from her chaperone to the vehicle. Although she had millions she'd never experienced something as trivial as a horse and carriage ride. She could go anywhere and do anything but it was always the smallest things in life that brought her significant amounts of joy.

"Hello, I'm William and I will be your driver this wonderful evening." The white bearded man spoke with a British accent.

"What's up, Will?" Tyson responded with a nod.

"Pleasure to meet you, William." Treasure smiled.

"Sir, Madam," he nodded to each of them, still holding open the door.

Tyson held Treasure's hand up to give her some balance as she stepped up the steps into the carriage. Once he climbed in behind her William closed the door and walked around to the other side, hopping in. He gave the thick black leather leashes a good thrashed and hollered *Yah.* Right after the carriage was set in motion; the clicking of the horses' hoofs could be heard as they moved forward and drove along. William's head was on a swivel as he took on the sights of the city.

THESE SCANDALOUS STREETS

Treasure looked up into the sky and it was the prettiest dark blue with a half a moon. Sprinkled around it were stars that twinkled and resembled crushed diamonds. It was beautiful, serene, and tranquil. The absolute perfect setting for romantic moment that Tyson was playing up. *Blip!* An eerie sound brought her attention around to her date who was now filling two flutes with some very expensive champagne. When he was done he sat the bottle down between his legs and passed her one of the glasses.

"Tyson, this is so, so astonishing." her head moved about as she took on the streets and the people occupying them. Everything seemed so different from where they were perched. It was like they were looking at the world through different eyes.

"How'd you put this together in such a short time?" she looked to him with a pleased expression.

He took a sip of champagne and shrugged like it wasn't a big deal. "I called in a few favors."

"Showtime!" they said to each other at the same time, busting up laughing throwing their heads back.

"You know what I always wanted to do?" she asked, savoring the taste of the alcohol on her lips.

"What's that?" he threw his head back and smacked his lips savoring the taste as well.

"The thing they do in movies where they hook their arms around one another and take a sip of their drinks."

"Hey, there's no time like the present." He curled his arm out and she curled hers around his. Staring into one another's eyes they took a sip from their respective glasses. They chuckled and she smacked her hand over her mouth to keep from spitting the champagne out. They wiped their chin with the back of their hands.

THESE SCANDALOUS STREETS

"You're a persistent ass nigga you know that?" Treasure smirked.

"Yep. I know what I want and I won't stop until I get it."

"Yeah?"

"Hell yeah." He replied confidently.

"Well, what is it that you want with me?" she took a sip of champagne.

"I want chu to be mine, my woman." He spoke with assurance, his eyes bleeding intensity and seriousness. "I don't know what it was but from the moment I saw you I knew that God had put chu on this earth, especially for me. I've never been sure of anything as I am at this moment. Facts." He took a sip from his flute.

"A man that knows what he wants in life and ain't scared to go get it."

"Sho' right."

"You plan on sharing that blanket with me handsome?" she looked to the thick plaid wool blanket.

"Sure do. Hold this for me." He passed her his glass and spread the blanket out over them. They then snuggled up next to one another and stared up at the sky. They were supposed to go to this tenement that Showtime owned and have a candle light dinner upon the roof, but ended up staying in the carriage talking the night away. The two of them discussed any and everything that came to mind. They discovered that they had quite a bit in common. Their hopes, dreams and future plans were almost the exact same. In the next five years they both could see themselves settled down with a family. As the night winded down Tyson found himself dozing off. His head dipped to his chest a couple of times before he threw it back up and blinked his eyes. Looking around he saw that they were back in front of the hotel. Glancing to his right he found Treasure sleeping peacefully with her head lying up against his shoulder. A smirk enveloped his face seeing her at ease.

"Well, here we are, sir." William said before jumping down into the street. He adjusted his apple jack and made his way around the vehicle. As he held open the door, Tyson scooped his lady up into his arms and carried her down the small steps. She stirred and smacked her lips before throwing her arms around his neck. He kissed her tenderly on the forehead and tipped William a fifty dollar bill.

"Thank you, sir." He lifted his hat above his head and gave a slight nod.

"Welcome." Tyson nodded back and carried Treasure toward the mansion. Entering her bedroom, he laid her down and sat down beside her, admiring her beauty as she slept. He then caressed her cheek and placed a kiss as gentle as a rose petal on her forehead before approaching the door. Opening it, he turned around to give her another look before continuing out of the door and closing it to.

Twenty minutes later

Treasure stirred awake and her eyes settled on the ceiling as thoughts of Tyson invaded her mind. She was feeling him but didn't want to make the mistake of giving her heart to someone who didn't treat it like the fragile object it was. She had her heart broken once before when Trip was murdered and she wasn't sure if she could deal with it again. See, she'd be taking a risk fooling around with Tyson. Things could go either way with him. The way she saw it she could end up with the greatest love she'd found since her late boyfriend or the greatest heartache she'd discovered since his death. But then again life was a gamble full of risks and the stakes were high. Some things would go in your favor and some would

THESE SCANDALOUS STREETS

not. What you envisioned to be your dream could become your nightmare. But sometimes you had to say fuck it and let the chips fall where they pleased. It would be better to take a chance and see what would happen instead of doing nothing and wondering what may have been. She deserved to be happy again and reasoned that Trip would have wanted the same for her. See, she knew that if she were up there in heaven instead of him, she'd want him to move on with his life and enjoy it while he could.

Treasure hopped out of bed and took a quick shower. Her naturally long hair was curly having gotten wet so she put some gel in it so it would keep with that appearance. Afterwards, she applied makeup to her face and slipped on a pinstriped button-down shirt, playing up her cleavage. She then picked up the bottle of Chanel Coco Mademoiselle and sprayed her neck and wrists. Her pretty bare feet made their way across the bedroom floor and stopped at the door, taking hold of the knob. She looked up at the ceiling and said, "God, if this is a mistake, please give me a sign to stop what I'm about to do."

Treasure closed her eyes for three minutes waiting for a sign from God Almighty, but it never came. "Alright, here goes nothing," she blew hard and opened the door. Tip toeing over to Tyson's bedroom door, she turned the knob and crept inside. Treasure stepped into the doorway of the bathroom and found Tyson lying back in a tub of hot water with his eyes closed, relaxing. Sitting down on the edge of the tub, she reached down in the water and grabbed his manhood, startling him. His eyes popped open and he swung a .45 around into her face, its length of it dripping wet. With her freehand, Treasure gently lowered his head bussa and he put it away. He lay back in the tub and closed his eyes, allowing her to stroke his dick to its full potential. Treasure was impressed by his length and girth. Her small French manicured hand went up and down his meat, starting off slowly but eventually speeding up once she saw him nearing his climax.

"Ahhh! Ssssss! Ahhh!" Tyson's eyes rolled to their whites and his mouth hung open, he looked as if a supernatural entity had possessed him. He licked his lips and stirred around in the water. Although, he felt himself about to bust he held back as long as he could being that Treasure's hand felt so good. He fought the inevitable for a while longer but evidentially the singer's gentle touch and grip got the best of him causing him to skeet everywhere.

"Ah, sheeiiiit!" Tyson cursed and his body twitched as he shot off like an AK-47 with an extended magazine. He looked up at Treasure like a hungry tiger, biting down on his bottom lip sensually. Catching her off guard, he pulled her into the tub with him, button-down and all. They kissed rough and hard, as if they were thirsty and their mouths produced the sweetest nectars. He unhooked her bra, freeing her melon size breasts from captivity. They were perfect; round and symmetrical. Taking one into his palm, he sucked on its dark brown nipple like a newborn baby, drawing a hiss from her pouty lips. Next, he took a hold of the other breast, showing it just as much attention as the first one.

"Ahhhhhhhhh!" The sensation sent a current of pleasure through Treasure's body, causing her to shudder and throw her head back. Ready to feel his steel all up inside of her, she stood up in the tub and removed her panties, while he tore open the gold foil wrapper of a magnum condom. He rolled the rubber down to the end of his shaft and then took a hold of her succulent thighs, guiding her onto his swollen mushroom tip. Squeezing all of him into her wet grip, she howled from a combination of pain and pleasure. "Oooooh!" It took

THESE SCANDALOUS STREETS

a while before she was use to his girth, but once she was broken in; she went for broke, riding him like a mechanical bull. He tried to take control but she wasn't having it, she smacked his hands away.

Smack!

It had been a while since she had sex and she wanted to prove to herself that she could still bring it.

Treasure grinded hard onto Tyson shaft, moving her hips as if she was in a hula hoop, round and round. It got so good to her that she moaned and clawed at his chiseled chest, causing him to hiss like a rattle snake.

"Sssssss! Ahhhh!" He expelled, eyes squeezed shut and jaws squared.

Treasure's jaw dropped as she worked him even harder, nearing the orgasm she'd been suppressing for the past five years. He took her hands from his chest and pulled her into him, bracing her body against his own; he pumped her feverously until they both came. Exhausted, she laid her head against his chest, smiling in satisfaction as she gently bit his peck. They giggled as they stared into one another's eyes.

Their sexual escapade continued into the bedroom. This time it was Tyson that put it on Treasure, though. About thirty minutes later they lay in bed in each other's arms.

"That was great." Treasure told him, circling his peck with a nail. Her other hand propped up her head and she stared lovingly into his eyes.

"Great?" Tyson frowned. "Frosted flakes are great, that was fucking fantastic."

"Okay, fucking fantastic." She turned his head towards her and sensual kissed him. "What happens next?"

"What do you want to happen next?"

"I want you to keep it one hundred with me, Tyson," She sat up in bed, looking dead ass serious. "'cause I'ma keep it one hundred with you. What happened tonight can stay a friendly fuck and we can both move on and act as if it never happened. But I cannot and will not be a jump off 'cause…"

"Shhh," Tyson hushed her, putting a finger over her lips. "I know you aren't like that and I'm not just looking at this as a one nightstand. To be honest with you I don't know where this is going, but if something does blossom beyond this night I think it would be beautiful. Let's not rush to put labels on things, let's just take things as they come and see how they play out, you good with that?" Treasure nodded yes and he kissed her, their mouths groping one another passionately.

Treasure straddled Tyson, kissing on his chest she said, "Can I get one for the road?"

"Can't get enough, huh?" he smiled arrogantly.

She laughed. "Not when it's good. No."

He rolled her onto her back, positioning himself for an encore of his phenomenal performance.

Twenty minutes later

Treasure stood outside of Tyson's door kissing him.

"Let me go before we get started again," Treasure said, wiping spit from her mouth with the sleeve of her shirt.

"Alright."

"Nice to see y'all two made up." A voice said from behind Treasure. She turned around and was surprised to see Skylar there with two flutes and a bottle of Chardonnay.

"Sky, what're you doing sneaking up behind people?" Treasure questioned.

"Ain't nobody sneaking up on y'all," She assured her. "I've been standing outside your door for the past five minutes knocking. I needed someone to drink and watch

THESE SCANDALOUS STREETS

Gone With the Wind with." She smiled. "I see you finally let Sexual Chocolate in them guts, huh?"

"Bitch, shut up."

"Oh, I ain't hating, please believe that boo boo. Gone and get yours. God knows you need it." Skylar put her out there. "Good looking out, Ty. My homegirl needed that, she ain't had none since..." that was as far as she got once Treasure muffled her mouth with her palm. With her freehand Treasure opened the door to her room.

"I'll see you in the next few hours." Treasure told Tyson.

Tyson smiled and nodded, seeing Skylar still trying to talk with Treasure's hand over her mouth as she backed her into her room and closed the door.

Later that day

Tyson and Skylar stayed behind in the car while Treasure entered the building to see her father. After standing in line for thirty five minutes and going through all of the shit they put visitors through to see an inmate, she was finally permitted to see her father. The room was a cluster of chatter. It reminded her of the auditoriums throughout school. You'd hear an ensemble of voices; individual students would be having a conversation of their own until the curtains drew apart and it was time for the show to begin.

Treasure sat at a table on a bench looking around at all of the people who were already talking to their loved ones or eagerly waiting to see them. Her eyes scanned over the faces of the inmates that flooded the visiting room, searching for the one that belonged to her father. Just when she thought all of the inmates that were coming into the visiting room had entered, in waltzed her father. Grief strolled in like he owned the place. His swagger and the aura surrounding him screamed boss. And though he was one of the smallest cons in the correctional facility, he was also one of its most influential. Treasure stood to her feet seeing her father approach. She smiled and they embraced. Grief stepped back and took a good look at her. She'd usually visit him once a month but lately with her touring schedule and all of the responsibilities that came with her celebrity status, he hadn't seen her in a couple of months.

After exchanging pleasantries they sat at the table with Grief holding her hands in his.

"There's something different about you." Grief turned his head at an angle trying to figure out what had changed about his daughter.

"Well, I have lost a lil' weight." She informed him.

"Nah, there's something else." He leaned back to take her all in. "You're glowing. Who is he?"

"What?" she blushed, trying to conceal a smile.

"Don't *what* me, girl. I'm your father. I know when there's a man in the picture. I haven't seen you beaming like this since you brought Trip home. What's his name?"

"You already know him."

"I do? Who?" he raised an eyebrow.

"Tyson."

"Tyson? The cat I sent up there to protect you?" he asked surprised. She nodded yes. "He is a good looking young man. I guess I should have been expecting that one."

"I know it's sketchy. I wasn't expecting for it to happen. It just did. We're taking it slow, but if you feel some type of way about it, I'll let it be."

"Nothing in my life means more to me than my baby's happiness. If you see something in this boy and you wanna see where it goes you have my blessing." He kissed both of her hands and she smiled.

THESE SCANDALOUS STREETS

Grief and Treasure went on talking until a CO's voice boomed over the loudspeaker telling the inmates that their visit had came to a close.

***

Cody moved toward the telephone booths with an easy bop, navigating his way through a sea of convicts, getting head nods from some and mad dogs from others. He noticed Whispers in the far corner listening to what one of Grief's goons were telling him but keeping his hateful eyes on him. Abruptly, Whispers balled his hand into a fist and stuck out his thumb, dragging it across his neck. This was his way of letting Cody know that he was a dead man. Once Grief's goon saw what he was doing, he mad dogged him as well. The youngster twisted up his face and chucked up the middle finger, moving on about his business.

Since the day that Tyson was set free he'd been shooting icy daggers his way. Although he knew that his cousin had brokered a deal so that he wouldn't be harmed while he did his time, he still felt uneasy whenever the seasoned convict was nearby in the facility. His paranoia had gotten the best of him. He could feel it in his gut that drama was bound to pop off between them which was why he played the prison with a shank stashed in his asshole.

Cody's bid had been pretty much smooth sailing since his cousin's departure. Niggaz stayed the fuck out of his way since they knew that he was under Grief's protection. His homeboys that had left him for dead when trouble came knocking at his door tried to come kick it once they heard that he was good money with the Bay Area shot-caller again, but he wasn't having that shit. Hell to the mothafucking naw. In fact he broke all four of their punk asses off for leaving him high and dry like that. They didn't dare to retaliate because they knew that they would be met with extreme violence if they harmed so much as a hair on his head.

Cody snatched up the receiver and brushed it off on his shirt. After punching the numbered buttons, he pressed the telephone to his ear and turned his back to the wall. His eyes moved all about until they found Whispers who was still watching his ass. Right then he began plotting his demise because he'd be damned if he let his ass get him before he met with death at the end of his shank. A slight smirk formed at the corner of his lips when he heard a voice come on the line.

"What it is, relative?" Tyson came on the telephone.

"Ain't shit, maintaining." He watched Whispers and the goon leave the corner, watching him with angry eyes. He switched the phone to the other ear and threw his hand up, striking a pose like *What's cracking, nigga?* Whispers nodded and gave him a look that he read as *I got something for your ass.*

"Grief's people watching your back up in there?"

"Yeah, they're looking after me."

"I'ma send you a lil' something, alright?"

"Good looking out, reli. I sho' 'nough appreciate it."

"Don't wet it, we're fam."

"Right, right, right, how you doing out there, though, loved one?"

"It's cool." He reported. "I'm just doing my job and making this money until they release my nigga, you feel me?"

"Can't be mad at that."

"Straight up. Well, look, I got some shit I gotta handle so I gotta get outta here but you make sure you get back up with me when you get that."

THESE SCANDALOUS STREETS

"Alright, love you, C."
"Love you, too."
"Peace."
    Cody hung up the telephone and took a deep breath. With his phone call out of the way, he moved forth and got lost in the sea of convicts. He didn't know when Whispers was going to get at him but he was going to prepare for him. That's for damn sure.

THESE SCANDALOUS STREETS

Chapter Thirteen

Malakai sat at the kitchen table stuffing his face with black eye peas, mustard greens, yams, corn bread and short-ribs smothered in gravy. He sucked the gravy from his fingers and took a drink of his grandmother's homemade lemonade. Sitting the glass down, he got right back to business.

Mrs. Williams sat at the opposite end of the table watching her grandson devour the meal she'd prepared for him. She cracked a grin. He looked up at her staring at him.

"Why are you staring at me like that, momma?" he smiled.

"You look so much like your brother right now scoffing down that food. The resemblance is uncanny." Her voice cracked with emotions and her eyes pooled with tears. "God knows I miss that boy." She wiped away her tears with the back of her hand.

Malakai wiped his mouth with napkins. He walked over to his grandmother and wrapped his arms around her. He lovingly kissed her on the cheek and pressed his cheek against hers. "I know, momma. I miss him, too." He dabbed the tears that cascaded down her face with a tissue.

Mrs. Williams blew her nose in the tissue and said, "You know I went to see the police chief a while ago and they're doing nothing to apprehend his killer? My grandbaby was shot down in streets like a damn dog and these people who have sworn to protect and service us can care less." She shook her head shamefully.

Knocks at the door grasped their attention.

"I've got it, momma." Malakai headed for the door.

"Who is it?" Mrs. Williams turned around in her chair.

"Showtime." He replied looking through the peephole.

THESE SCANDALOUS STREETS

He unchained and unlocked the door. As soon as he pulled it open he was greeted by Showtime's infamous smile. The Big Willie Records founder lowered his shades, revealing his yellow cat eyes. The contacts coupled with his gold capped fangs made him look like a serpent.

"I know that ain't Kai? He said excitedly. "What's happening?" he slapped hands with him and they embraced. "When you touch down, daddy?"

"Couple of days ago."

"Word? Well, let me hit chu off with a lil' something 'til you get back upon your feet," he reached into his suit for his money-clip.

"Nah, I'm good, fam, cats been throwing dough at me since I came home."

"Alright, then. You remember Keith, don't chu?" he motioned towards the expressionless bodyguard.

"Yeah, what up?" Malakai threw his head back.

"'Sup?" Keith said in a less than friendly tone.

"Y'all have a seat," Malakai motioned to the living room as he closed the door shut. "Can I get y'all anything?"

"A 7up, if you have it." Showtime answered.

Malakai looked to Keith who said, "I'm good."

"How are you doing, Mrs. Williams?" Showtime asked as she walked over with the support of a cane and sat down on the sofa.

"I'm fine. Thank you." She replied unpleasantly.

Showtime ignored it and tried another approach.

"Lovely day isn't it?"

"I wouldn't know I haven't left the house yet."

Malakai sat a can of 7up on a coaster before the CEO of Big Willie records.

"Thanks." Showtime reached into his suit.

THESE SCANDALOUS STREETS

"You're welcome." He replied, sitting next to his grandmother.

Showtime placed an envelope on the coffee table and pushed it in front of Mrs. Williams. Picking up the 7up, he leaned back in the chair and cracked it open. He took a drink as he watched Mrs. Williams slide on her glasses and open the envelope. Inside there was a check for $250,000 dollars; every month Mrs. Williams would receive a check hand delivered by Showtime on Blessyn' behalf. Before the late rapper had met his tragic demise he'd signed all of his royalties, including his business dealings over to her. Mrs. Williams was the overseer of his estate.

"That's a nice healthy check, Mrs. Williams," Showtime told her. "Don't go spending it all on champagne and strippers now." He laughed and nudged Keith, who forced a slight smirk. Mrs. Williams wasn't the least bit amused, though.

She removed her glasses and massaged the bridge of her nose. She then looked to Showtime and said, "Do me a favor."

He sat up in his chair and said, "Anything."

"From now on mail my checks to me. This is the last time I want to see you..." she turned to Keith, twisting her face, and looking at him like he was dog shit beneath her shoe. "...or your flunky in my home, understand?"

A look of confusion appeared on Showtime's face. He looked to Keith then back to Mrs. Williams. "I'm sorry, Mrs. Williams, was there something that I said?"

"No, sir, there's something that you've done." She glared at him.

"I'm afraid that you've lost me. What is it that I've done?"

THESE SCANDALOUS STREETS

"Oh, I'm sure you both know." She looked to Keith then back to Showtime.

"Momma, you're tripping." Malakai asked concerned.

"Hush, boy! The greatest trick the devil ever played was convincing the world that he didn't exist! But I know he's alive and well, 'cause he's sitting before me now in my living room!" her eyes became red and glassy. She clenched the handle of her cane so tight that everyone could have sworn they heard the wood cracking.

"Sorry about all of this, Showtime." Malakai apologized sincerely on the behalf of his grandmother.

Mrs. Williams dropped her cane and got to her feet clutching, clutching The Holy Bible to her chest. She pointed two fingers out at Showtime, like she was about to cast a spell. "I cast thee outta my home demon, this is a house of the Lord, leave here and never return!"

"That's our cue, Keith." Showtime rose to his feet and gave Malakai his business card. "Get at me if you need anything."

"Alright, Show. Sorry about this again, my nigga."

"Don't wet it, my G." he slapped hands with him.

Malakai closed the door behind his guests and turned back around to his grandmother. "Momma, what's gotten into you?" he asked concerned.

"That man has something to do with your brother's murder. I'm telling you I can just feel it in my bones, son."

"What? Momma, Blessyn was killed during a carjacking so how do you figure he had something to do with it?"

"Believe half of what you see and none of what you hear," she told him with a firm expression. "The devil is a master of deceit and manipulation."

Malakai massaged the bridge of his nose and shook his head. "Alright, ma, I gotta go."

THESE SCANDALOUS STREETS

He pecked her on the cheek, grabbed his jacket, and headed out of the door.

Meanwhile

"Yo', man, I think grandma suspects something." Keith told Showtime.

"Maybe so; she can babble all she wants, though. Nobody will believe her. She can't prove a thing."

It was eleven o'clock at night when Blessyn pulled up to the park banging Scarface's Smile in his purple Lamborghini with the peanut butter interior. He executed the engine and hopped out clad in camouflage fatigues and matching cap, swagged the fuck out. He took a drink of his lemon Snapple as he advanced in Showtime's direction, his iced out cross and Jesus piece swinging from left to right. The lights of the park hit the jewelry and made its diamonds twinkle like the stars in space.

Blessyn stopped before Showtime and took another drink of his Snapple. He screwed the top back on the bottle and slapped hands with the CEO of his label.

"What's up, fam?" he addressed him.

"You know the streets are talking," Showtime began, massaging his chin with a jeweled hand. "And they're saying you're severing ties with Big Willie after this next album." He cleared his throat with a fist to his mouth. "Now, I'm not one to take what a few niggaz say and run with it 'cause that aint never been my style. Nah, I'd rather hear it straight from the horse's mouth."

Blessyn looked him dead in his eyes without so much as blinking an eye. "Yeah, I plan on making a move." He spoke as if it wasn't a big deal.

THESE SCANDALOUS STREETS

"Say what?" the multimillionaire's forehead wrinkled. He couldn't believe that one of the biggest stars on his label was saying that he was about to cut out on him especially since he'd given him his big break.

Blessyn looked Showtime dead in his eyes, speaking loud and clear. "After this next joint I'm out. I took a few meetings with A1 Entertainment and they're talking about: two albums, 1.5 mill. I keep all of my publishing and my masters."

"So, you leave me to find out about it like this, through word of mouth?" Showtime asked hurt, eyes having grown glassy. He looked at the rapper like he was his little brother so this revelation cut him deeper than any scalpel could. "I thought me and you were 'pose to be better than this. I thought we were family."

"I was gone tell you, my nigga, but with us celebrating this new album going double platinum. And seeing how happy you were, I didn't know how to come at chu about it, ya feel me? I was just waiting for the right time for us to sit down and chop it up, real spit."

Showtime nodded and gripped Blessyn's shoulder, placing his hand on the back of his neck. "Come here." He managed a weak smile as he embraced him, tears streaming down his cheeks. "You broke my heart," he whispered into the rap star's ear and pecked him on the cheek. Right after, he shoved him backwards and walked off.

Hearing movement at his back, Blessyn whipped around and met a dark figure. He held his arm over his brow trying to see the face of who it was standing in the darkness, straining his eyes. Abruptly, the mysterious person pointed something at him that he couldn't make out but his heart told him that it was a gun. Realizing that his life was in danger, Blessyn's eyes bulged and he gasped.

THESE SCANDALOUS STREETS

Poc!

"I'm telling you, nephew. You should let me run back up there real quick and put that old bird outta her misery." Keith said, holding the door open for his boss.

"Nah, leave it be," Showtime hopped into the backseat and he closed the door shut behind him. He looked up at the complex that Mrs. Williams resided in. In his head he ping ponged the idea of going back up to her place to waste her.

Tap! Tap! Tap!

Showtime tapped on the window with his huge platinum ring for his uncle's attention. He turned around.

"Come on, man. Let's go."

Keith rounded the Maybach to hop behind the wheel. His plans of murder would have to wait.

***

Malakai jogged from the complex his grandmother resided in and hopped into the front passenger seat of Dameekia's Range Rover. The truck was white with black leather interior and 24 inch black rims with chrome lips. After slapping hands with Bizeal and Crazy who were sitting in the backseat, he looked from the stuffed Betty Boo hanging from the rearview mirror to the rest of the vehicle. He nodded his head in approval, pleased with his lady's vehicle.

"This is a nice lil' ride you got here." He complimented her.

"Thanks, babe." Dakeemia smiled as she pushed the behemoth, Chloe glasses covering her eyes, hair wafting in the wind like a T-shirt hanging from a clothes line. She was happy that her man liked her whip.

"That crip nigga hooked my boo up, huh?" Malakai looked over his shoulder to Bizeal and Crazy, who nodded in agreement. Out the corner of his eye he noticed the smile had disappeared from his lady's face. "What? Chu thought I didn't know you were messing with that nigga from Harlem while I was holed up? I ain't wetting it. I told you once I was sentenced to do you out here as long as you didn't fuck with nobody I knew. You needed somebody to hold you down and I sure as hell couldn't do it caged up." He took time to light a cigarette and punched the cigarette lighter back into its rightful place. Next, he took a pull and then blew smoke. "That shit dead now though, right?" She nodded yes. "Good, 'cause you're gonna drop this mothafucka off to him once I'm done getting my usage out of it. My bitch can't be pushing a ride the next nigga bought her. Once I make this move I'ma lace you and have you whipping some European shit straight off the showroom floor, ya feel me?" She conceded. "Just trust and believe in your nigga. I got this. I got us." He proclaimed, smacking his chest.

That night

Blat! Tat! Tat! Tat! Tat! Tat! Tat!
"Gahhhh!"
"Ahhhh!"

The men danced on their feet as bullets passed in and out of them. Their bodies went crashing down to the floor alongside several others that were scattered over the linoleum marinating in blood. Romadal looked up from where he was at the top of the steps with two M-16s held up at his shoulders. He was dressed in a robe and cheetah print draws. His forehead was sweaty, his eyes were bugged, and his mouth was hanging open. He focused his attention on the entrance of the mansion. The first mothafuckaz that came through that door was going to get set on fire with jacketed

THESE SCANDALOUS STREETS

bullets. Romadal wiped the perspiration from his forehead with the sleeve of his robe and adjusted his weapons, pointing them at the floor near the door.

He breathed heavily and his heart leaped behind his chest causing his peck to twitch. Swallowing the lump of nervousness in his throat, he trained his eyes on the mouth of the mansion. His palms were sweaty but he was able to keep his grips on the handles of his assault rifles.

"Come on, come on, you cock suckas!"

For a time there was silence and then abruptly, Bizeal tucked and rolled through the door. He came up from the floor, AK-47 clutched, finger squeezing the trigger. The assault rifle rattled and spat heat at the kingpin. He returned fire back, backpedaling up the spiral staircase, with his eyes squinted. Slugs were flying around his head and body, tattering the wall behind him and knocking down portraits.

"Ahh! Ahhh! Ahhh!" Romadal threw his head back hollering and collapsing to the steps, having taking a few in the arm. He cradled his limb to his side but kept a strong hold on his M-16, crawling towards the top of the steps. He looked from the door of his bedroom to downstairs where he saw a masked up Bizeal and Crazy moving in on him, AKs held low at their sides ready to stop a nigga's heart from pumping. The kingpin got to his knees. Hunched over with bullets flying over his head, he retreated to his bedroom and slammed the door shut behind him. He pressed his back up against the door grimacing. Looking to his arm he saw that it was mangled and bleeding profusely. "Aww, shit!" he blurted taking inventory of his wounds. His head snapped up when he heard a loud crash and the shattering of glass. Malakai swung in through the large window of his bedroom on a zip line dressed in black fatigues and wearing a neoprene mask on the lower half of his face. Before Romadal could lift his M-16, some hot shit was bursting his chest open like a bag of potato chips.

"Arrghhh!" He grimaced and another rush of pellets flipped that ass like a D-boy with a strong hustle game, leaving him strewn on his stomach. Malakai moved in on his kill, eyes and an automatic shotgun focused on him. He approached with caution, kicking his assault rifles from out of his reach. Next, he kneeled down and placed his hand to the pulse in his neck, it was gone. From there he stood erect looking for the place he was told that the kingpin stored his weight. Knocks at the door drew his attention to it; he strategically approached it being sure to stay out of its path where bullets could leave him flat-line. He leaned up against the side of the door holding his shotgun up at his shoulders, turning his head toward the door before speaking.

"Who is it?" he hollered out, slightly muffled by the mask covering his nose and mouth.

"It's us, nigga, open up!" Bizeal hollered back.

After stealing a glance through the peephole and seeing that it was his niggaz, Malakai unchained and unlocked the door. He pulled it open and they poured in, eyeballing the homie that he'd dispatched on the floor bleeding out.

Click! They looked up hearing the door closed behind them and finding their leader there pulling a map out from the confines of his jacket. He pulled the neoprene down from the lower half of his face and opened the map, kneeling down to the carpet with it. They both stood over his shoulder as he looked from the map to the wall where the entertainment center resided. A smile broadened his face when he realized that specific area was where his prize was stored. Standing up, he drew the axe from around his back. The others followed suit, withdrawing their axes as well. He

THESE SCANDALOUS STREETS

patted the back of the metal into his palm, studying the space where his reward was stashed.

The threesome moved the entertainment center aside and Malakai pressed his ear up against the wall, knocking on it. Once he heard the hollow space he smiled triumphantly. Thereafter, he and his niggaz went to work and attacked the wall with the axes vigorously. Grunting as they hacked away at it and sending plaster flying everywhere. After a time beads of sweat began to form on their brows but they kept at it until they were staring dead at what they had come there in search of: blocks of yay, weed, and heroin. Malakai threw his arms over his nigga's shoulders they stood admiring the fruits of their labor. They smiled and laughed, throwing phantom punches at one another, ecstatic about their new found fortune.

After cramming their prizes into the sacks that they'd brought along, they stashed the fruits of their labor away and left the scene in a hurry.

"You got 'em baby?" Dakeemia asked her as she sped off the grounds of the mansion.

"Got 'em, baby, gimme some lip." He cracked a smile and turned his thick lips to her. She kissed him.

Malakai pulled his small notepad from his back pocket and took a pen from out of the console. He crossed out the last name on his list Romadal. The Sheridan was now his. But little did he know that he'd left two unknown witnesses inside of the mansion would eventually become his downfall.

THESE SCANDALOUS STREETS

Chapter Fourteen
The next day

Tyson and Dead Beat stood on the roof of Big Willie Records passing a smoldering blunt between them. Tyson looked down upon the city's people wondering where they were going and whether they'd get there. He watched as some got into taxis and mounted motorcycles and bikes, while others drove their cars or walked. He rapped the hook to Tupac Shakur's *California Love* featuring Dr. Dre.

"All Eyez On Me," Dead Beat named the album the song appeared on. "That song and that video went in hard."

"Yeah, I remember the video; they were on some Mad Max Thunder Dome type shit." He hit the blunt and passed it back to the beat maker.

There was a moment of silence and then Tyson spoke again.

"So, how long have you been down with Showtime and his camp?"

"Man, let's see," the white boy scratched his temple and thought on it. "About seven years now. I met his nephew Styles while I was in 'hab. He liked what he heard and slid my instrumentals to him."

"Hab?" Tyson raised an eyebrow, not sure of what he was talking about.

Dead Beat put the blunt in his mouth and rolled up the sleeve of his button-down, exposing the track marks from his days of a heroin addict. Those days were long gone but the fading scars still remained. He wasn't the least bit ashamed of them. He wore them as if they were badges of honor; medals he was rewarded for war. The war he fought against his demons for repossession of his life.

"Oh, rehab." He nodded.

THESE SCANDALOUS STREETS

"Yep," Dead Beat rolled his sleeve back down and buttoned the cuff.

"I take it that you've worked with the late great."

Dead Beat nodded yes and then blew out a roar of smoke. "I've done Blessyn's entire catalog," he counted the albums off on his fingers. "Prince of the Ghetto, Redemption, Brave Heart, God's Blessyn, and this new joint we're working on, Thug Angel. I've done all of your girl's albums, too. On this new project she's supposed to bring in other producers, though." He passed the blunt off.

"Like who?" Tyson asked before hitting the blunt.

"Timberland, Dr. Dre, Kanye and Pharrell, I think."

"That's a hell of a line-up. I know it's gon' be some heat on there."

"Yeah, me jumping on a project with these cats is gonna make me go harder. I've gotta show them this white boy from Virginia got something in his bag. Don't get me wrong my resume is nice and dudes know I put that work in. But I'ma be on an album with some heavy weights. And when fools hear Treasure's new shit I want them to be like, 'Damn, these cats went in but that white boy ain't nothing to fuck with.' You feeling me, dawg?"

Tyson nodded and blew out smoke into the air. "All day."

Dead Beat picked up his bottle of Hennessy from the ground and poured himself a cup. "You want some of this, Ty?"

"Nah, I'm good. I'm on the job. Really shouldn't be fucking with this." he held up the blunt.

"My bad, dude. I'm tripping. I forgot you're Treasure's guy." He poured a little Coca Cola into the cup to mix with the Hennessy.

"What up with lil' momma? She gotta dude?"

THESE SCANDALOUS STREETS

Dead Beat looked up at him with a big smile. "You're checking for Treasure G, huh? Nah, she doesn't have a guy. Hell, I can't remember the last time I saw her with a guy that wasn't on Big Willie's staff."

"For real?" Tyson couldn't wrap his head around how a woman as fine as Treasure didn't have a man in her life. It had to be something seriously wrong with her to keep a guy from wifing her up.

"Scout's honor," Dead Beat crossed his fingers and took a sip from his cup.

"What is she a hermaphrodite? She gotta disease or something?"

Dead Beat laughed. "Nah, Treasure is all woman, believe me I know. I accidently walked in on her when she was getting out of the shower. It cost me a smack across the face but you won't hear any complaints."

Tyson smiled. Treasure did have a sick ass body. "Then what's her damage?"

"Treasure hasn't been involved with anyone since her dude was murdered. From what I hear he was the last guy that claimed her heart. The way Showtime tells it the cats that rocked him to sleep did him something nasty. His people couldn't even have an opened casket funeral." He shook his head and took a sip from his cup. "But you didn't hear that from me."

"I gotchu."

"Look, don't get me wrong, Treasure's a diamond in the rough. But once you peel off those outer layers and smoothen her out you have a jewel worth holding onto forever. Feel me?"

"I know y'all ain't up here getting blazed without me." Skylar came through the roof's door. She approached the fellas and Tyson handed her the L.

THESE SCANDALOUS STREETS

"Drink?" Dead Beat held up the bottle of Hennessy.

"Yeah, I do the Hen-Dog," Skylar told him, ready to get a taste of the dark liquor. "What y'all up here talking about?"

"Life and the people in it," Tyson informed her.

"Would this convo happen to include my girl?" she smirked.

Tyson smiled and said, "Maybe. Is she still down there with that journalist from Source Magazine?"

"Yep." She tried to pass the L back to Tyson.

"Nah, I'm good, slim. A nigga gotta be on point. Matter of fact let me go down her with your girl."

As Tyson made a beeline for the roof's door, Dead Beat and Skylar peeked over the ledge at a UPS van that had just pulled up in front of the building. The delivery man loaded a box onto a dolly and rolled it into Big Willie Record's building.

"What chu think he's got in there?"

"If Showtime ordered it, you can bet it exceeds the imagination." He passed her a cup of Hennessy.

***

Treasure sat with Jillian Arnold, the journalist from The Source doing an interview. She was to be featured on the cover of the popular hip-hop magazine for promotion of her upcoming album *Forever Me*.

"How long have you been singing?" Jillian asked Treasure. She sat before her with an ink-pen and pad with a tape-recorder on the glass table top.

"Forever and a day," the crooner laughed. "I'd say since I was about seven years old. I'd stay glued to the tube waiting for a Mary .J Blige to come on. So I can sing into my brush like it was a microphone. It's all so surreal to me how

THESE SCANDALOUS STREETS

this started out as a dream, but through hard work and determination I turned it into a reality."

"Now, I understand it was Showtime that discovered you outside of an Arco gas station in your home town. He said you were out there slinging your mixtape, *God's Gift,* out the trunk of your car like they were bootleg movies."

"True. I was out there rain, sleet, or snow with my CDs tryna create myself a lil' buzz. I figured if I created a strong enough of a following that the labels would come knocking on my door. But I got lucky and ended up running into Showtime. Yes, it was Showtime that took my CD, but it was Blessyn that pressed him to listen to it. I like to give them both credit."

"Okay. I know it's kind of personal but I have to ask because I'm sure the fellas out there want to know, 'Are you single and ready to mingle, or are you taken?'"

"No. I'm happily single. I've yet to find the right guy to put a ring on it." She held up her hand and wiggled her ring finger.

"Wait a minute, girl," Jillian looked at her like she couldn't believe her. "You mean to tell me that delicious scoop of chocolate I saw you walk in here with isn't your man?"

"I take it you mean Tyson." Treasure smiled, cheeks blushing. "No. He's my bodyguard." She lied not wanting the media all up in her business. It was bad enough that they were following her. They'd really be up her ass if they knew that she had a love interest now.

"Take it from me, girl, if he's a keeper you better snatch him up. You'd be surprised what you can find right under your nose. I've been with my husband twelve years now, and when I tell people he'd been my mechanic four years prior they can't believe it. He'd asked me out a million times and

THESE SCANDALOUS STREETS

I'd shot him down every one. Thank God that man was persistent and I finally gave him a chance, because now I know what it truly means to be happy." Treasure nodded her head. "Look at me babbling on, is there anything you'd like to say before we wrap this up?"

"Yes. Be on the lookout for *'On My Way Home'* dropping September 26th. It's gonna be bananas. Shouts out to my label Big Willie Records; Showtime I see you. Keith, I love boo, and big ups to my management, Money Making Moves Management. East Oakland I got us."

Jillian stopped the tape-recorder and said, "Okay. That's it." She stuffed her items into the black leather briefcase and rose to her feet, embracing the singer. "Thanks for letting us do this interview with you."

"Thanks for blessing me with the cover."

Jillian broke their embrace and stared Treasure in the eyes. "You remember what I said, okay?"

Treasure nodded yes and headed for the elevators. She pressed the *up* button and stepped inside once the doors parted. The doors were almost closed when a UPS delivery man stuck his foot between them and rolled a box in on a dolly.

He looked to the numbered buttons for the floors and then to Treasure. "Looks like we're headed to the same floor, huh?"

"Yep, is that addressed to Jarvis Spears?"

He checked his clipboard. "Yes. Hey, aren't you that singer, what's her name? Treasure Gold?"

"That's me."

"Say, you mind signing my cap?"

"Sure. As long as you don't mind me being nosy," She nodded to the box.

"Oh, I have no idea, I just make the deliveries."

THESE SCANDALOUS STREETS

"Right, what's your name?"

"Gus." He held up his nametag, which was embedded on his shirt. Treasure signed his cap and gave it back to him. "Thanks."

"You're welcome, Gus."

Ding!

The elevator doors parted and Treasure stepped out behind the UPS delivery man. She ran right into Tyson who was getting off the other elevator.

"Hey, I'd just left the lobby looking for you."

"You must've just missed me. I wrapped the interview up a minute ago." She looked over his shoulder at the delivery man who'd just rolled the box into Showtime's office.

Tyson turned around. "What're you looking at?"

"Come on, I wanna know what's inside of that box he brought into his office." She pulled him along with her down the hallway. She knocked on the door of Showtime's office and he stuck his head out a moment later, cracking the door so only his eye could be seen.

"What's up, T?"

"What chu got inside that box, nigga? And why are you cracking the door open like you don't know me?" her brows furrowed.

"Top secret Big Willie Records shit, but don't trip you'll find out soon enough." He slammed the door in her face before she could say another word.

Treasure looked to Tyson like *I can't believe he just did that.*

About ten minutes later Showtime called for everyone to come inside of his office. Moments later his office was filled with Big Willie Records staff and artists. He threw himself back upon his marble desk top and picked up the compact

THESE SCANDALOUS STREETS

remote beside him. He pointed the remote at a black device. A green light flashed on it and it projected a very lifelike image of the late great rapper, Blessyn. He was a tall, cornrow rocking brother of a brown complexion. He was slim but had well defined muscles. His body was littered with tattoos. The one most noticeable was the one scrolled across his stomach in Old English letters, *Thuggin'*. The rapper had a microphone in his hand spitting the lyrics to his song *You Gotta Feel Me*. Gold jewels hung from his neck and wrists. His diamonds were dripping, he was icy as fuck.

Thought niggaz was my homies but they ain't right/ four shots in the dark tryna take my life/Lying bleeding in the streets I seen the light/Gotta daughter on the way I can't die tonight/ Put my faith in the Lord, I'm in your hands/ Blessyn you're not dying it's not in my plans/ Took the slugs out my frame then he healed me, man/ sent me back to the streets told me kill it, fam/ Keep it real 'Hard to Kill' tatted over my wounds/ say I'm crazy than a motha, a thugged out loon /Looking for those cowards that shot me, loading them slugs/out for payback, homie, I'ma take it in blood...

After the hologram was done rapping, Showtime turned it off. "So, what y'all think?"

It looked so real, like it was really him." One staff member said.

"Yeah, it does. It's so surreal." Another staff member said. "How much did it run you for, Mr. Spears?"

"I can't tell you all of that, Playboy," Showtime cracked a gold fanged smile and then lit a cigar, blowing out smoke. "I'ma drop this Thug Angel project and take the hologram out on tour. I think I'll call the tour Night of the Living Dead." He smiled and licked his lips, nodding at his marketing plans. "We'll film the concert and release it along with the CD. I stand to see some real paper off this next album."

THESE SCANDALOUS STREETS

Not everyone was feeling Showtime's idea. The whispers amongst the audience made this obvious.

"That's Showtime, anything for a buck."

"Blood sucking vampire."

"This nigga going straight to hell."

The millionaire mogul caught wind of some of the less than flattering comments and decided to clear his office. "All right, show's over, y'all get the fuck outta my office!" He opened the door and shooed everyone out except Dead Beat, Skylar, Treasure and Tyson. Afterwards, he slammed the door so hard that it rattled the portrait of Blessyn hanging on the wall above his desk.

"This is wrong, Jarvis." Treasure voiced her opinion with a frown.

"You wanna run that by me again, baby girl?"

"What you're doing is wrong. You're exploiting a dead man."

"I'm not exploiting anyone, sweetheart, Blessyn signed a contract with me for five albums, after Thug Angel his contract is fulfilled." He dumped ashes into an ashtray.

"You wanna drop another Blessyn album? Fine. But don't parade his image out on stage like he's some puppeteer for a couple of dollars. For God's sake, Jarvis, what will his grandmother think?"

"As long as she receives her check every month she shouldn't have shit to say. Mrs. Williams gets enough loot to keep her ass in minks, gold, and Mercedes Benzes, baby. Blessyn made sure that woman was well taken care of before he checked out. May he rest in paradise."

Treasure shook her head, looking at him disgusted. "It's all about the money with you, isn't it?"

"Cha-Ching."

THESE SCANDALOUS STREETS

"Fucking asshole," She stormed out of his office with Skylar and Tyson on her heels.

Treasure barged through the double glass doors of the Big Willie Records building outside onto the sidewalk. She leant against the establishment.

"You all right, Treas?" Skylar asked concerned.

"I'm fine. I could use a drink though."

"Dead Beat has some Hennessy. Do you want me to get chu a cup?"

"Please." Treasure fished around in her purse for her pack of cigarettes. After she found the pack, she pulled one out. She tried to light it but she couldn't produce a flame. "Shit." She cursed, throwing the lighter aside. "You gotta light, Ty?"

"Yeah," He produced a lighter from his pocket and sparked up her square.

Treasure took a pull and blew a cloud of smoke into the air. She wiped the tears from the corners of her eyes and said, "God look at me, little Miss Ghetto Diva out her crying like a lil' bitch."

"Sometimes crying is the best medicine." Tyson spoke with a seriousness plastered across his face. "Shedding a few can be the perfect remedy."

Treasure smirked, looking up at him like she couldn't believe what he'd just said. "Is that your philosophy?"

"It's the truth."

Showtime came through the double glass doors and approached Treasure. He stood directly in front of her, but she didn't acknowledge him. She continued to smoke her Joe while looking through him as if he were transparent.

"I'll leave you two alone." Tyson headed back into the building.

THESE SCANDALOUS STREETS

"So what's up, T?" Showtime addressed his songstress. "You don't have any more love for ya boy?"

Treasure expelled smoke from her mouth and into her nostrils, and then said, "Fuck you, Jarvis!"

"Look, baby girl, I know you may think I'm some blood sucking leach. But I'm doing this to keep my man's memory alive and to make sure his people are eating. I know that's the way he would have wanted it so that's what I'm gone do; even if it makes me look like a horned demon to folks, smell me?"

"Aye, you don't have to explain yourself to me. It's your artist and your label, you can do whatever the fuck you wanna do...*pimp!*"

"Treasure, come on, now. This is me right here. You know me. I would never try and play Blessyn like that. The man was not only my artist but my brother. Does this look like the face of a man that would do anything crafty?" he pouted his lips and batted his eyes. Treasure couldn't help but to crack a smile. "Show me some love." He opened his arms. They embraced and he pecked her on the cheek.

Camera flashes from Showtime's left stole his attention from Treasure. He turned around and found a paparazzi snapping away.

"Yo, my man, can't chu see me and the lady are having a moment?" he asked aggressively, nostrils flaring. The paparazzi ignored him and continued taking pictures. "Get outta here, homie. Gone now; beat it!" He grabbed the bulge in his slacks and shook it at him. This didn't bother the pap though, he kept busy. "Oh, you must think I'm playing with you huh, bitch?" he sneered.

Treasure grabbed his arm. "Come on, Jarvis, let's get outta here."

THESE SCANDALOUS STREETS

Showtime snatched away. "Nah, fuck that, this nigga think it's a game."

The multimillionaire charged the pap. He snatched the camera from his hands and shoved him to the ground. He then slammed the camera into the side of the building until it crumbled into pieces like a stale cookie. "You saw the suit and tie and thought a brotha went soft. I'ma show your pale narrow ass corporate thugging." He kicked the pap in his side, cracking his ribs. He then proceeded to stomp him out like Robert De Niro did Billy Bats in Goodfellas.

Tyson, Skylar and Dead Beat came running out of the building but by then the damage had been done. Showtime pulled a money-clip from his suit. He took half of the bills and was about to give them to the pap, but changed his mind and threw all of the money on him.

"There you go; settled out of court." He adjusted his tie and turned around.

"Yo', Show, are you all right, fam?" Tyson asked with a wrinkled forehead.

"Yeah," he draped his arms over Tyson and Treasure's shoulders. "Let's go get something to eat; it's on me."

***

Nearly the entire Big Willie entourage fell through to Roscoe's Chicken & Waffles. They ate heartily and shot the shit. Once everyone had gotten good and full they moved out and headed in their separate directions. While Skylar and everyone else took it to King Henry's gentlemen's club, Treasure and Tyson decided to take it back to the mansion.

They came through the door kissing, rubbing and touching, accidently knocking over a nearby vase when they crossed the threshold. *Crash!* The vase shattered on the floor, breaking into pieces.

"Aw, shit!" Tyson looked down at it.

"Shhh," Treasure hushed him with her finger to his lips.

"Shhh, my ass," Tyson told her, worrying. "I'ma have to pay for that, and I know it's a few grand sitting up in this place. How much this mansion cost, 4.5?"

She laughed. "Don't worry about it; I'll take care of it. And Preston will clean it up in the morning."

Treasure took Tyson by the face and kissed him, hard and passionately. They made out going up the stairs and into her bedroom, where he fell on top of her on the bed. He removed her Steve Madden sandals and pulled off her skinny jeans. Using his teeth, he pulled her panties down, revealing her bald vagina. Tyson stood face to face with the pussy like a boxer would his opponent in the center of the ring before a heavyweight championship fight. He took his time admiring it, as if it was the painting on the ceiling of the Sistine Chapel. It was hands down the most beautiful love-box he'd ever laid eyes on. He looked from her pussy to its owner who was giggling and smiling. He smiled back. Holding her legs apart, he brought his hot, wet mouth to her sex, penetrating it with his tongue and allowing it to slither between her walls. Treasure flinched and hissed. Closing her eyes, she allowed Tyson to make love to her with his mouth. His oral skills took her to a paradise of pleasure she had no idea existed. The Low Bottom's thug had the princess of R&B Soul talking in tongues. He couldn't believe his ears, the jargon sounded like the language Martians used to communicate with one another. Her moans let him know that he was handling his business, which drove him to work her clit even harder.

Tyson brought his head up from Treasure's honey pot

THESE SCANDALOUS STREETS

trailing a length of saliva from it to his lips. He wiped his mouth with the back of his hand and looked to her V. It was oozing with her juices and jumping at the same time. Her thick caramel legs shook uncontrollably. He smiled at his handiwork, thinking the Pussy Monster had struck again. Tyson stood to his knees, unbuckling his red belt and unzipping his camouflage cargo shorts. He pulled his boxer-briefs down exposing his erection. His dick was so hard that it damn near touched his stomach. He'd barely gotten the condom on before Treasure had grabbed his hardness and guided him inside of her.

"Mmmmmm." His eyes rolled and he shuddered, even through the rubber he could feel the warmth and moisture of her sex. He moved his love muscle in a circular motion at a slow and steady pace, and then he hit her with the long strokes. Pushing and pulling his thick length from her wound.

"Ahhhh, ssssss." Treasure's eyes fluttered as his girth massaged the walls of her slickened tunnel. He'd grind in her passionate rhythm and pull back until only the tip of his dick was inside of her before pushing all of him back in, going balls deep. Only his nut sack would be hanging out of her. A sheen of sweat formed on his forehead as he laid it down. The sheen of sweat soon turned into beads as he worked Treasure from his side, holding up her right leg and forming a human scissor.

"You like how that feels, baby?" he asked with slit eyes, his face was that of a man who'd just entered Heaven.

"Yesssss." She spoke sensually with a grimacing face and shut eyes, feeling his hardened meat sliding in and out of her aisle of love.

"Grrrrr!" His brows furrowed and he clenched his jaws, showcasing his teeth. Feeling himself about to explode, he

THESE SCANDALOUS STREETS

gripped her hips so tight that she winced. His slow and steady pace had increased and he began to pound her with such intensity that he soon shot his load. "Ughhhh!" Tension released his body like a pair of strong hands and relief washed over his face. Exhausted, Tyson laid his head against her back. He sweated, smiled and panted all at the same time. "Haa! Haa! Haa! Haa!"

Treasure turned over in bed to face her lover. He grabbed her hand and brought it to his lips, kissing it as he stared into her eyes, happily. She stared back into his with a fulfilled expression. Suddenly, seriousness came over her.

She cleared her throat and began, "Tyson."

"Yeah?" he asked, eyes closed as he gently kissed her hand as if it were her lips. She curled her finger and tilted his chin up so that he'd be looking into her eyes. "What's up?" a line formed across his forehead when he noticed the dead ass look on her face.

"Call me crazy but I think…" she looked down as she trailed off.

"You think what?" he encouraged her, tilting her chin up like she'd done his. Staring into her face he could tell that she was quite nervous which made him eager to hear exactly what she had to say.

"I think…I think I'm in love with you."

"That's funny 'cause *I know* I'm in love with chu."

They both smiled and shared a long, deep, sensual, loving kiss.

Meanwhile in another room of the mansion

A dark figure sat before half a dozen TV monitors drinking Cognac over the rocks having just watched Tyson and Treasure's sexual escapade. The blue glow of the monitors

THESE SCANDALOUS STREETS

illuminated his face. He wore a sinister smile, pleased with what he'd seen. He pressed *Stop* on the *VCR* and *ejected* the video-tape. After labeling the tape he placed it into a safe along with other others. Some of the labels they wore were: Treasure peeing, Treasure taking a shower, Treasure masturbating, Treasure undressing, Treasure oiling her body, etc. The dark figure had the mansion wired for sound and had hidden cameras installed in every room. It wasn't anything he didn't know about the people that had lived or stayed at the estate.

He closed the safe and cut the light out in the room.

***

Cody was in a wife beater and homemade doo rag while down on his knees inside of his cell. He moved down the cold filthy floor wiping it down with a hot soapy rag, careful not to miss a spot. As he moved along he could see his reflection on the floor. It was almost as if he was looking into a mirror. Hearing footfalls nearing his house he peered up to see Whispers and a host of niggaz. Cody stood up on his knees and felt his stomach drop below him. He was nervous but the scowl masking his face put up one hell of a front. See, he refused to buckle in the face of fear. Homeboy was spawned from a rare breed of gangstas.

"What's up witchu, C-Doggy Dog?" Whispers cracked an evil smile.

"What's bracking?" Cody prepared himself for what may very well be the fight for his life. He knew that this day was coming and here it was.

THESE SCANDALOUS STREETS

Chapter Fifteen

Malakai sat with Dakeemia and the rest of his crew at a table inside of an Italian restaurant called Rizzo's. Everyone was decked out in their best for the special occasion. They'd all turned out to celebrate the young hustler's new found success as a young boss. Before they'd hit up the restaurant they visited a casino called The Lucky Charm, and Dakeemia had cleaned up at the crap table.

"A bitch sitting nice and pretty." Dakeemia smiled and thumbed through the dead presidents she'd won at the crap table.

"What chu gon' buy ya man?" Malakai lit up a cigar and fanned out the flame of his match he'd struck it with.

"Whatever he want." she leaned over and kissed his lips. They both cracked smiles but they faded once they heard the manager.

"I'm sorry, sir, but there's no smoking in here." He informed the young hustler. Malakai pulled a few Benjamins from his Armani suit and placed them into the breast-pocket of the manager's blazer. The manager smiled and said, "Well, I'm sure we can make an exception for the night." before walking away.

"Money talks and bullshit walks." Dakeemia commented, stashing her winnings into her Hermes bag and pulling out a tube of MAC, applying it to her thick, juicy lips.

"With that said, I don't want chu climbing them poles at that flesh factory. Yo' man's home now. That ain't no place for a hustler's wife. You gone have niggaz thinking I'm not taking care of you."

"You weren't tripping off of it being a flesh factory when I met chu in there. I told you I'm not like the rest of these hoes that are content with having their niggaz take care of

THESE SCANDALOUS STREETS

them sitting up on their asses. I like being able to do for myself and take care of my own. Besides, you do enough for me as it is. You've given me the world, boo."

Malakai took her by the chin, looking in her eyes he said, "Sometimes the world is not enough." before kissing her. When he pulled away she was smiling goofily like she was drunk off of his kiss. "As of tonight you're no longer employed at King's, you hear me?"

"Yes, baby, gimmie another kiss." She grabbed him by the side of the face and kissed him deep and passionately.

"Aye, don't chu see me and my date are tryna eat?" Bizeal said with a mouthful of Zidi.

"Get a room." His date laughed, wiping her mouth after guzzling red wine as if it were a 40 oz bottle of Olde English 800.

Still kissing the hustler and Dakeemia held up a middle finger to Bizeal and his date.

Crazy tapped his wine glass with his dinner fork, *Tink! Tink! Tink!* "May I have your attention, please? I'd like," he burped. "I'd like to purpose a toast," he burped again, holding his fist to his mouth. "Damn. Excuse me, my bad, dawg. I'd like to purpose a toast to my nigga Malakai, my brother from another, here's to our success. Let's take this game by storm and live our last days as kings." Everyone touched glasses and sipped the wine. "Now, I'll perform the twenty-one gun salute in his honor." He spoke with a drunken slur, whipping his head bussa from his suit. He went to hold it up toward the ceiling and his date stopped him.

"Baby, not in the restaurant." Crazy's date told him.

"This nigga Crazy, boy," Malakai shook his head before taking a sip of wine.

"Man, have you lost your rabid ass mind?" Bizeal frowned at Crazy. Seeing him about to take the bottle of

THESE SCANDALOUS STREETS

wine to the head, he snatched it from his hand. "Uh huh. No more alcohol for you, homeboy. You've had enough for the night."

Everyone laughed.

Thirty Minutes Later
Malakai and Bizeal each had one of Crazy's arms over their shoulders as they helped his drunken ass through the double glass doors of Rizzo's. The girls brought up their rear. When they made it outside their chauffer, who was leant against their limo taking a smoke break, dropped his cigarette to the sidewalk and mashed it out under his cheap patent leather shoe. He stepped to the back passenger door and opened it.

"Yo, y'all holding?" a haggard looking fiend inquired, scratching his neck. He was in a tattered white T-shirt that was stained yellow around the collar and dirty jeans that had tears at the knees.

"Tyrone, you need to bounce, you see where the fuck we at?" Bizeal asked heatedly.

"Oh, my bad, but a nigga out here jonesin," the fiend's mouth moved like he was chewing something but it was empty. He needed a fix badly. "I'm tryna cop a twenty, but I'ma couple dollas short, can you help me out?" he pulled out a few crumbled bills and some loose change from his pocket.

"You believe this nigga?" Bizeal looked to Malakai then turned back to Tyrone. "I'm not gonna tell you again, homeboy. Bounce or get bounced, mothafucka!"

"Alright, look," Tyrone stuffed his money back into his pocket. "What if I had some information for you? I'm talking about some real top secret shit." He rubbed his hands

THESE SCANDALOUS STREETS

together and looked around cautiously, making sure that no one was watching him about to sell his bit of knowledge.

"You got Crazy, man? 'Cause I'ma 'bout to put the beats on this nigga." Bizeal looked to Malakai with a hard face. He was dying to put them hands on him.

"Nah, chill lets' see what he has to say." He looked to the crack head. "Speak, nigga, and you bets not be wasting my time."

Tyrone looked around to make sure no one was listening to what he was about to say. "I know who it was that smoked your folks."

"Who?" the hustler's brows furrowed. His crew had splattered many niggaz around the city during the war for control of drug territory, but they had yet to have any casualties on their end so he wondered who these *folks* his smoked out ass was talking about.

The fiend leaned in closer so only Malakai could hear him. What was said pissed him the fuck off. He frowned and squared his jaws. Murder flashed in his eyes and he busted the crack head in his mouth. *Bwap!* Specs of blood flew as he went sailing backwards into the limo, sliding down to the sidewalk. "I see you gotta death wish." He looked around to make sure no one was watching him as he whipped out his head bussa, cocking one into its chamber. Tyrone's eyes bugged and he wished he would have kept his mouth shut. It was too late now. The nigga should have never parted his goddamn lips. Malakai threw open the backdoor of the limousine and pulled his scrawny black ass inside, dazed and moaning. Bizeal came right behind him, closing the backseat door shut as he climbed inside.

"Go ahead, nigga, say some more fly shit, so I can give you a vasectomy." Malakai dared the crack head, pushing his gun into his crotch. His eyes were wide and glassy as he

THESE SCANDALOUS STREETS

looked down to the steel pressed into his crotum then into the eyes of the man holding it. They were dark and madness dancing in them.

"I'm serious, man. I could tell you!" the junkie was frightened.

"Tell 'em what?" Crazy slurred, climbing inside the limo. He looked from the smoker to his homeboy, gripping his shiny black tool.

"Shhhhh!" Malakai held a finger to his lips, hushing his friend. His eyes never wavered though. Nah, they were concentrated on who he deemed was the biggest piece of shit to have ever been oozed from between a woman's legs.

"Man, this fool done wet himself." Bizeal frowned, seeing the wet spot expanding at his lap.

"Ugh." Crazy turned his head in disgust.

Looking into the hustler's eyes, Tyrone knew he meant business. He wanted to back pedal and say what he knew was just word of mouth, but then he'd be gambling with his manhood. And with a 40 .cal underneath his nut sack he wasn't willing to try his luck. Swallowing hard he decided to tell the upstart all that he knew. "Okay. I'll tell you…"

Malakai brought his ear to the crack head's lips, listening attentively to what he was being told. After adhering the story his eyelids snapped open and his mouth went slack.

"What's up, Mal?" Bizeal frowned.

"Fuck he say?" Crazy's face twisted.

Malakai drug Tyrone out of the back of the limousine, letting him drop to the pavement hard. He winced when he bumped the back of his head on the sidewalk but scrambled to his feet hastily. He was about to run when the crack peddler snatched him back by the collar of his shirt, ripping it a little further. *Schhhhrippp!* He forcefully turned him around so that he'd be facing him. Staring deep into the

THESE SCANDALOUS STREETS

windows of his soul he said, "Get the hell outta here and don't chu breathe a word of what chu just told me to anyone! Ya hear?" his face contracted with anger and he gritted, shaking the crack head by his collar, causing his head to bob violently.

"Yeah! Yes!" Tyrone swallowed his spit and nodded his head rapidly.

"Get the fuck outta here!" he kicked him in his ass as he made to run off. He fell out in the middle of the street, scrambled upon his feet and took off running.

Urrrrrrk! Honkkkk!

A Toyota pickup truck nearly hit his bony ass but he managed to escape unscathed.

***

A yellow Crown Victoria pulled upon a block that resembled a ghost town. The community looked just as spooky as the one in the original Exorcist movie with its fog. It was dark save for every other light post dimly illuminating it. There wasn't a soul out except for the cat hopping out of the cab. After paying his fair, Tyrone turned around and looked up at the house he was supposed to meet the man that was supposed to pay him. Once the cab drove off, he pulled a piece of paper from his back pocket and unfolded it. He looked from the paper to the address on the house, his brows wrinkled. The house barely looked habitable especially with it windows boarded up and the grass that was knee high. Thinking nothing of it, Tyrone tucked the paper into his pocket. He licked his dry chapped lips and rubbed his calloused hands together greedily, thinking about the handsome reward he was to receive.

THESE SCANDALOUS STREETS

He walked into the yard and jogged up the steps upon the porch. Once he lifted his fist to knock a sharp whistle drew his attention. His forehead furrowed and his head snapped around to the left, his fist lingered in the air. From within the recess of the shadows he saw a dark figure wave him over. Tyrone hustled down the steps and came around the side of the house. There he met a cat in a big black hat and a trench coat that was tied tight around his waist; his hands were tucked in his pockets. The crack head narrowed his yellowing eyes and leaned forward trying to see the face of the mysterious man.

"Did you tell 'em what I told you to?" the man's voice came through a distortion device.

"Yeah." Tyrone nodded, rubbing his hands together, ready to be blessed. "I told 'em exactly what you told me to tell 'em, nothing more nothing less."

"How'd he take it?"

"He was shocked; shidddd, how you expect 'em to take it with what I laid on 'em?"

"Right, right." He nodded his understanding.

"Well, you got my blessing?" his eyes were bugged and his mouth was salivating thinking about the treat he was in for.

The man reached inside of his trench coat and pulled out a Ziploc bag full of tan crack rocks. Before he knew it the fiend was snatching the bag from out of his gloved hand. He hurriedly pulled a black scorched and scratched up glass stem from out of the small pocket of his jeans. The mysterious stranger watched as he stuffed the stem with rocks and set fire to the end of it. The drugs sizzled and crackled as the bluish orange flame cooked the crack inside of the glass. He sucked on the end of it blowing puffs of thick white smoke.

THESE SCANDALOUS STREETS

Tyrone became so occupied with getting high that he wasn't any longer paying the stranger any mind.

"I trust that this whole thing stays between us?" he gave him a look like *You better say yes.*

"Yeah, yeah, yeah." The junkie closed his eyes and tilted his head back, blowing out a cloud of smoke. He wasn't trying to do much more talking. All that lip service was starting to bring his high down.

"My man, you have a good one." The mysterious man patted him on the shoulder as he passed him.

Ssssssss!

The rocks sizzled as they were cooked at the end of the stem. Tyrone was holding the flame of his lighter to the glass and sucking on the opposite end of it.

Choot!

The top of Tyrone's head splattered and he hit the ground hard. *Thud!* The man extended his gloved hand down at the twitching fiend and exercised his trigger finger.

Choot! Choot! Choot! Choot!

He lowered his weapon to his side. After he took the time admire his handiwork, he brought his head up and looked around. His white breath misted the air as he breathed heavily. The mysterious man dropped his gun beside the lifeless body. As he turned to walk away he pulled his collar up to combat the cool air.

***

"What's up, man?" Bizeal inquired.

"What that nigga tell you?" Crazy wanted to know.

Malakai leaned up against the limousine with his head hung, running his hand down his face. He looked like he had been dealt the most devastating news in his life. His eyelids

THESE SCANDALOUS STREETS

stretched wide open, lips forming a tight line; he blew hot air from his nostrils.

"Babe," Dakeemia placed a comforting hand on his shoulder, a concerned expression written across her face. "What did that crackhead tell you?"

Finally, Malakai lifted his head and looked at his girl. "I know who murdered my brother."

To Be Continued...
These Scandalous Streets 2

THESE SCANDALOUS STREETS

AVAILABLE NOW BY TRANAY ADAMS
The Devil Wears Timbs 1-7
Bury Me A G 1-5
Fear My Gangsta 1-5
The Last of The Ogs 1-3
King of Trenches 1-3
The Realest Killaz 1-3
These Scandalous Streets 1-3
A Hood Nigga's Blues
A Gangsta's Empire 1-4
A South-Central Love Affair
Me And My Hittas 1- 6
The Last Real Nigga Alive 1-3
A Hood Nigga's Blues
Bloody Knuckles
Fangeance

COMING SOON BY TRANAY ADAMS
Bloody Knuckles 2
They Made Me An Animal
Dope Land

www.ingramcontent.com/pod-product-compliance
Lightning Source LLC
LaVergne TN
LVHW010325070526
838199LV00065B/5649